Book Two
Crimson Veil

Truth bleeds deeper than guilt.

Contents

Chapter One: The Net Tightens

The morning news buzzed from the outdated TV perched above the bar in the corner of the station. Grainy footage played on a loop—students dancing under red lights, shadows twisting, faces blurred, but not entirely unrecognizable. Debbie's face flashed up again: "Missing: Last seen near city centre. Any information, please call—"

Detective Inspector Laura Halstead stood silently, coffee in hand, eyes fixed on the screen. There was something about this case that itched beneath her skin. The students were closing ranks. Faculty was tight-lipped. Something had gone wrong in Nottingham, something darker than a missing person.

Across the city, Mike sat at his kitchen table, still in his boots from the night before. The house was quiet, save for the slow hum of the fridge. The spot where Debbie had once lain was now scrubbed raw, the scent of bleach still faint in the air. He hadn't slept. He hadn't even tried.

Mary had called earlier, but he let it ring. He didn't want calm voices or clever planning. He wanted action. He wanted the silence to break.

A knock at the door made him flinch. He reached for the blade he'd started keeping in the drawer.

"Mike," came a familiar voice. Jane.

He opened it cautiously. Her face was pale, her dark eyes alert. "They were at the Uni today. Questioning students. Looking for inconsistencies."

He stepped aside and she entered. "How bad?"

"Bad," she said. "They've asked for phone records. CCTV pulls. One of Amy's friends was talking—loose-lipped, scared. Said something about blood rituals, some kind of secret society. They're getting close."

Mike let out a low exhale. "And what about the video?"

"It's everywhere," Jane said bitterly. "Clipped. Muted. Just enough to stir the pot. The press is hungry."

At that moment, his phone lit up. A message from Mary: "Emergency meet. 6 PM. Same place."

"They're circling us like wolves," Jane said. "And we've got no pack leader."

Mike stared at her. "Then maybe it's time someone stepped up."

Across town, Mary was already at the meeting spot—a dusty, disused room above a shuttered bookstore they'd used for their original gatherings. She paced, tapping her phone against her palm, thinking, planning.

The door creaked and Mark entered, hoodie pulled up. He didn't say much, just nodded.

They were trickling in, one by one, faces tighter than before, eyes hollower. The unity they once celebrated felt fractured. The thrill had turned sour.

When Mike arrived, the room shifted. He walked in with purpose. Not the reluctant participant anymore. Not the bystander.

"We need to be smart," Mary began.

"No," Mike interrupted. "We need to be ready." He scanned the group. "The police aren't going to stop. We all know that. So we have a choice. Run. Or fight."

"Fight how?" Jane asked, arms folded.

"Information," Mike said. "We find out what they know, how far they've come. We take control of the narrative."

"And if they already have too much?" asked Mark.

Mike's eyes darkened. "Then we make sure they don't live long enough to use it."

Silence.

The game had changed.

Chapter Two: Through the Cracks

Detective Inspector Laura Halstead rubbed at her temples as the overhead lights of the incident room flickered slightly. Sleep had become a stranger in recent days, replaced with caffeine and a dogged determination that only the truly obsessed could understand.

Across the table, Detective Sergeant Arun Malik was scrolling through security footage, eyes glassy from hours of screen time. Halstead walked over and handed him a second coffee. He took it with a grateful grunt.

"We're missing something," she muttered.

"No signs of forced entry at the hotel," Malik replied. "And none of the staff remember seeing Debbie that night. But..." He tapped the space bar, pausing on a frame. "There's this."

The image was grainy but clear enough: a man in a hooded jacket, walking away from the suite door. Time stamp: 03:17 AM. No face. No sound. Just a flicker of movement, and a shadow sliding something under the door.

"Envelope?" Halstead guessed.

"Looks like it. Can't tell who picked it up, though. No interior footage."

"Still," she said, "we have someone on the outside involved. That changes everything."

She returned to her board—a collage of printed stills, timelines, and scribbled notes. At the centre: Debbie Farrell,

22, third-year student, missing seven days now. Around her, a slowly growing web of names, locations, and digital evidence. A few had been officially questioned Amy, before her mysterious disappearance. Mark, who offered too little and too smoothly. Mary… That one didn't sit right. Too controlled.

"Where are we with the university records?" she asked.

"They're dragging their feet," Malik said. "Something about student privacy. Legal red tape."

"Then we lean harder. Someone's going to crack."

She turned to a new addition: a printed screenshot of a viral video. A short, six-second loop with blood, muffled cries, and a shrouded figure. No faces. Just implication. It had surfaced four days ago and exploded online. The tech team was working backwards, trying to trace the upload point.

"Anything from the metadata?"

"Wiped," Malik said. "Professionally."

Halstead's brow furrowed. "They've got someone smart on their side."

A knock on the door interrupted. A young officer entered, breathless. "Ma'am. You're going to want to see this."

He led them into the adjoining tech room. One of the forensic analysts had a laptop open, fingers poised dramatically above the space bar.

"We decrypted part of the message in that envelope," she said.

Halstead's pulse quickened.

The screen showed a scan of a torn piece of paper. Barely legible script. The analyst zoomed in and enhanced the text. Four words:

"She chose the knife."

Silence.

"Is that a confession?" Malik asked. "Or a taunt?"

"Could be either," Halstead said. "Or both."

She stared at it. The phrase was too calculated to be random. This wasn't about sex games or misguided rituals anymore. This was a game of power and control. Someone was orchestrating this like a play. Carefully. Sadistically.

"And get this," the analyst added. "We found a matching phrase posted anonymously on a dark forum three days ago. Same words. Same handwriting, scanned and uploaded."

Halstead didn't move. "They're playing with us."

"They're inviting us," Malik added quietly.

Halstead looked back at the photo wall. The faces, the timelines, the lies.

"No more cat and mouse," she said. "I want all of them on watch. Full surveillance. Let's see how they act when they feel the walls closing in."

Chapter Three: Pressure Points

Mike stood with his back to the kitchen sink, arms folded, eyes fixed on the group gathered around his dining table like students facing a final exam. The lights were dimmed, curtains drawn, and the air inside was thick with tension—cigarette smoke, unspoken thoughts, and a growing sense of dread.

"They've made it official," Jane said, breaking the silence. "Debbie's now listed as a missing person on the university site. Her picture is everywhere."

John swore under his breath and poured another drink. "It was only a matter of time."

"No," Mary said, coldly precise. "It was too late the moment we let that body hit the water. Now, it's just fallout."

Mike exhaled slowly. "And you think we can't manage the fallout?"

"Some of us aren't made for this," Mary replied, eyes flicking to Jane and Mark.

Jane looked small in her oversized hoodie, her leg bouncing nervously under the table. She hadn't been herself since Debbie disappeared. Gone was the flirtation, the hunger for pain and power. What was left was fragile, frayed.

Mark, as always, sat slightly apart from the others. He was hunched forward, fingering a torn beer label, not meeting anyone's eyes.

"We need a new plan," John said, pacing. "The cops are on us. I got stopped outside campus yesterday. Routine questions, they said. Bullshit."

"They're watching all of us," Mary agreed. "And they've probably linked us through Amy. She's vanished, which only makes us look worse."

"She hasn't vanished," Mike said sharply. "She's hiding. There's a difference."

"Doesn't matter," Mary snapped. "Every second she stays away, we look more guilty. They'll use her absence to divide us."

A moment of silence.

Then Jane spoke, voice trembling but clear. "What if someone talks?"

All eyes turned to her.

"I mean… what if they offer a deal? To one of us. If we turn on the others."

"They won't," Mike said.

"They will," Mary corrected, her tone icy. "They always do."

Mike walked to the table, his presence looming larger than the walls around them. "Let me make one thing clear," he said. "We're in this together. If any one of us cracks, the rest go down too. You think they'll show mercy? We're not just talking murder—we're talking desecration. Conspiracy. Obstruction."

"Jane didn't mean—" John started, but Mike raised a hand.

"She meant exactly what she said. And she's not wrong to be afraid. But if fear starts running this group, then we're already finished."

Silence.

Mark finally looked up. "So, what do we do?"

Mike's eyes narrowed. "We wait. We listen. We stay clean. That means no phones, no public meetups, no more mistakes. If any of you feel the need to confess your sins, do it to a priest. Not a detective."

Mary stood, gathering her coat. "Waiting won't save us. We need to get ahead of this. I've been following Amy's trail."

Mike's eyes narrowed. "You found her?"

"Not yet. But I'm close. She has the rest of that message, Mike. You know she does."

The room grew colder.

"If she turns it over to the police—" Mary didn't finish the sentence.

She didn't have to.

Mike looked around at the people he'd once trusted with blood and secrets. Now, he wasn't so sure any of them could hold under pressure.

"We find Amy," he said. "Before they do."

Chapter Four: Shadows and Smoke

Amy's boots slapped against wet pavement as she ducked down an alley off Mansfield Road, breath misting in the early morning chill. The city was still half-asleep, but she wasn't. She hadn't slept more than a few hours in days.

Not since the first video clip had surfaced.

Not since she realized someone else had been watching them too.

Nottingham was a familiar maze to her, but today it felt hostile. Every bus stop ad with Debbie's face on it. Every glance from a stranger that lingered too long. Every flashing blue light in the distance. It all set her nerves on fire.

She'd changed hostels twice. Paid in cash. Used stolen Wi-Fi from coffee shops to track mentions of her name online. So far, nothing direct—no formal charges. But the web was tightening.

And now, she was headed to Derby.

Not because it was safer—because it wasn't—but because she had a stash there. A burner phone, a hard drive, and the second half of that letter Debbie had been clutching when she died. She couldn't afford to leave any loose ends. Not anymore.

The 6:45 a.m. train to Derby was half-full. Construction workers, students, an old couple asleep by the window. Amy took a seat near the rear and kept her hoodie up, earphones in with nothing playing, just to signal silence.

She watched the countryside blur past and tried to slow her thoughts.

Who had sent that letter?

Who had recorded the video?

And most importantly—who else knew?

She was still asking those questions when she arrived in Derby. The city was waking up fast, people spilling into the streets like ants from a disturbed nest. Amy moved quickly through the back roads, avoiding cameras where she could, reaching the small storage locker she'd paid for months ago under a fake name.

Inside the locker was a black rucksack, dusty and untouched. She unzipped it and checked the contents:

A burner phone with one unread message.

A small, encrypted drive.

A clean set of clothes.

And the folded note she hadn't dared read until now.

Amy sat cross-legged on the cold concrete floor and stared at the envelope for a long moment. The same red wax seal. No name. Just a symbol—a crude drawing of a broken eye.

She peeled the wax away and unfolded the letter.

The handwriting was the same as the one Debbie had received. Sharp, elegant, and threatening in its precision.

"You've all played your parts well. But not everyone has been honest. The mirror sees what you deny. And the eye? The eye never forgets."

Amy felt her stomach twist. She read it again. Then a third time.

What the hell was this?

She powered on the burner phone. The unread message popped up in seconds.

UNKNOWN: You're running out of time, Amy. We see everything. You need to choose a side.

Her hand trembled. Not with fear—but with something close to rage. She was done running. If someone wanted to play games, fine. She could play too. And she knew exactly where to start.

Back in Nottingham.

She had one last stop in Derby—a cheap internet café near the university. There, she sent an encrypted message through a secure channel. Just three words:

"Meet me. Midnight."

She didn't sign it. Didn't need to.

If they were watching, they'd know where.

She stood, grabbed the rucksack, and stepped into the cold Derby air. Clouds loomed overhead, grey and swollen, ready to burst.

It was almost poetic.

Because Amy wasn't hiding anymore.

She was hunting.

Chapter Five: The Watcher

He watched them all.

From the quiet confines of his windowless flat, the Watcher leaned back in a worn leather chair surrounded by walls of monitors. Their faces blinked across the screens—Mike, Jane, Mary, Mark, and now, Amy.

Each one had played their role beautifully.

Each one had bled—some figuratively, some far more literally—for the cause.

The Watcher sipped from a chipped tea mug, the words Best Dad Ever faded to a soft blur. A memento from a life that had ended years ago. A past burned to ash by grief, betrayal, and one catastrophic night that no one else remembered anymore.

But he remembered.

He always remembered.

That's why the mirror in his flat was covered in black cloth.

Because what he saw when he looked at himself wasn't the man he used to be—it was the thing he'd become. The architect of this twisted ballet. The silent puppeteer pulling strings through coded letters, ghost accounts, and edited videos timed with surgical precision.

Amy had been easy to manipulate.

She always wanted to be seen.

Mike was predictable—military men always were. Guilt, pride, the need for control. He was the hammer.

Jane? Jane was the crack in the glass. Fragile but sharp when broken. And break, she would. Soon.

But it was Mary who fascinated him most. The queen on the board. Calculating, restrained, willing to do what the others wouldn't—because she believed she was above the rest. Because she'd buried her own sins deep in university corridors, hiding behind a polished smile and an old Oxford accent.

The Watcher ran his fingers across a keyboard, bringing up a live CCTV stream from the River Trent. He rewound two nights, paused, enhanced.

There.

The red glow of his decoy cam blinking on the bank.

They had seen it. Panicked.

And that had been the point.

Fear drives people to reveal themselves faster than truth ever could.

He opened another window—an email draft he had yet to send.

Subject: The Final Round

To: undisclosed recipients

Body: You've seen the warnings. Heard the whispers. Now it's time to choose. Tonight at midnight, the eye opens fully. One of you will not survive it.

He didn't send it.

Not yet.

First, he needed to check on the girl.

Amy.

He tapped a key and brought up a hidden camera feed—her student house in Lenton. Amy was packing. Nervous. Determined. He admired that about her. Despite the blood and lies, despite everything, she still had fight in her.

He respected fight.

But respect wouldn't save her.

He leaned forward, brushing aside a newspaper to reveal a carefully arranged set of items: a scalpel, a burner phone, and an ID card from the university. Not his own. Someone else's. Someone who hadn't been seen since last term.

Someone no one was even looking for yet.

"Time to finish the story," he whispered to himself

The story he had started years ago.

The story about how pain creates power. And power demands sacrifice.

He reached under the desk and pulled out a slim black case. Inside was an envelope—identical to the ones Amy and Debbie had received. Red wax, eye symbol, no return address

But this one wasn't going to any of the usual players.

This one was for someone new.

A wild card.

Someone no one expected

With a sharp flick of his wrist, the Watcher sealed the envelope and wrote a single name across the front.

SARAH.

Then he smiled, leaned back in the chair, and waited for midnight.

The hour of judgment was coming.

And this time, the blood would run deeper than ever before.

Chapter Six: The Rendezvous

Amy's boots slapped against the wet cobblestones of Nottingham's Lace Market, her breath fogging in the early evening chill. She pulled her coat tighter, the red envelope pressed to her chest beneath the fabric like a second, frenzied heartbeat.

The city glowed around her in puddles of amber and neon, but none of it felt safe. Every step echoed too loud, every passerby a possible tail. The messages had been cryptic—burn after reading stuff—but they all led her here.

"7:30. Beneath the old sign. Come alone."

She arrived outside the abandoned textile mill, the rusted iron sign still clinging to the brickwork like a rotted crown: ROWLEY & SONS — EST. 1881.

The place had been gutted years ago, a haven now for graffiti, rats, and— apparently—clandestine meetings.

Amy hesitated at the threshold.

Something about this felt... final.

She slipped inside.

The scent hit her first—wet wood, mold, and the iron tang of old metal. Shafts of moonlight spilled through gaps in the boarded windows, casting skeletal shadows across the floor. Her boots crunched over debris, but there were no voices. No sign of anyone.

"Hello?" she called, her voice too loud, too thin.

Then she saw it.

A single folding chair sat beneath a flickering utility lamp rigged to a power bank. On it, a mobile phone, face up, already recording. Amy stepped closer, heart thudding, and reached for it. As she touched the screen, it sprang to life.

A video began to play.

It was her.

Not from tonight. From the night everything went wrong.

The camera angle was high, maybe a ceiling corner—grainy, black and white—but there she was, straddling Debbie, the silver scalpel in her hand. Laughter from the group echoed in the background, blurred bodies moving in rhythm. Amy was smiling.

Until she wasn't.

Until Debbie's eyes rolled back, and the smile died.

Amy dropped the phone as if it had burned her. It clattered to the concrete.

A whisper drifted from the shadows.

"Do you remember what came next?"

She spun.

A figure stepped forward, cloaked in shadow, face obscured beneath a hood. Not police. Not Mike. Not Mary.

Not anyone she knew.

"What is this?" Amy demanded, her voice cracking. "Who are you?"

The figure stepped closer, hands open and unarmed. "I'm the one who's been watching. Guiding. Testing."

"Testing?" she barked. "Debbie's dead. We're being hunted. The group's falling apart."

"And yet, here you are. Alive. Resourceful. Dangerous."

Amy shook her head, stepping back toward the exit.

"You orchestrated this," she said, almost choking on the words. "All of it. The letters. The footage. Even the red light by the river."

"You all played your part," the Watcher said simply. "But only a few of you deserve to move on to the next phase."

Amy swallowed, her hand finding the envelope in her coat.

"What's in this?" she asked. "Why did you want me to have it?"

He gestured to the phone. "The key to your survival. If you're willing to use it."

"And if I'm not?"

A pause.

Then: "Then you'll be next."

The threat wasn't shouted. It didn't need to be. It was cool, absolute.

Amy stared at him, trembling. Not with fear— but fury.

"You have no idea who I am," she said. "I don't just survive. I endure. And I learn."

The Watcher tilted his head, like a curious animal.

Then, silently, he turned and walked back into the shadows.

Leaving Amy standing in a derelict building, phone still recording, red envelope still unopened, and her world tilting on the edge of something far worse than guilt or grief.

This was war now.

And she intended to win.

Chapter Seven: The Envelope

Sarah stood in her quiet kitchen, the hum of the old refrigerator the only sound.

The house had never felt more silent — or more threatening. She had just returned from her shift at the campus medical centre when she found the envelope tucked under her front door. No name, no return address. Just red wax, a stamped insignia she didn't recognize, and her heartbeat, picking up speed as she peeled it open.

Inside was a single photograph. Blurred. Grainy. But she recognized the faces. Hers among them — laughing, eyes lit in the glow of that infamous night at the hotel. A second image followed. Debbie, moments before she was found.

A note was scrawled beneath in dark ink:

"They all lied. Who will you protect?"

Her throat tightened. Sarah hadn't spoken to the others in days. Jane had gone quiet. Amy was missing. Mike — distant and harder than ever. Mary, always composed, now sending short, clipped replies.

Her fingers trembled as she picked up her phone. She started to type a message to Jane... then deleted it. What if this was a trap? What if someone was trying to pit them against each other?

A knock at the back door startled her. She jumped, heart slamming in her chest. She crept over, pulling the curtain back just a sliver.

No one.

But a second envelope had been left on the step.

She didn't open it right away.

Sarah stared at the second envelope like it might detonate if she touched it. Her breath came shallow and fast, her body frozen in place. The red wax was identical to the first—unmistakable. The same insignia pressed into its surface. A symbol she still couldn't place, though it stirred something in her memory, like a half-remembered dream—or a nightmare.

She finally opened the door, snatched the envelope, and slammed it shut again, locking it quickly behind her. Her fingers fumbled at the edge of the paper, and this time, the contents weren't photographs but typed pages. Five of them, carefully folded.

She laid them out on the kitchen table, her eyes scanning the first few lines. What she read made her stomach twist.

"The story you think you know is not the story that happened. The night Debbie died, you were all being watched. There are files. Recordings. Transcripts. What you did was only part of the performance."

"Check your inbox. They've started releasing pieces."

Sarah blinked, then sprinted to her bedroom and powered up her laptop. Her email loaded slower than usual—probably her nerves. Her university inbox showed a single unread message, subject line: The Curtain Rises.

The sender was anonymous, but the email body contained a single hyperlink and nothing else.

"No," she whispered. "This can't be happening."

Her fingers hovered over the mousepad. She clicked.

A browser opened to a private site with no branding, only a black background and a streaming video player.

The video began to buffer. Sarah's eyes widened as the image resolved: it was a timestamped video from inside the hotel suite. Low-light, grainy night vision. But the shapes... the outlines... the voices. She could recognize them.

There they all were. Amy. Mark. Jane. Herself. And Debbie.

There was laughter. Drinks. Tension.

Then a shadow moved across the screen— someone not in the group.

She gasped. "Who the hell is that?"

The figure's face never showed, but they moved with precision. Confident. Like they belonged there. The video skipped forward: Debbie entering the bathroom. Another skip. The shadow slipping in behind her.

Then... static.

The screen went black.

Sarah slammed the laptop shut, the sound echoing like a gunshot in the still air.

Her hands trembled. Her mouth was dry.

Debbie hadn't died from a game that went too far.

She was murdered.

And someone had been filming it all.

The knock at the front door nearly made her scream.

She grabbed a kitchen knife without thinking and crept slowly toward it.

Another knock. Soft. Three gentle raps.

She pressed her eye to the peephole.

Mary.

Sarah opened the door, just a crack.

Mary stood there, calm as ever, her coat dusted with rain. But her eyes were hard.

"We need to talk," she said.

"I just saw—" Sarah whispered.

Mary held up a phone. "I know. It's spreading. Someone's leaking the footage. Not just to us. But to everyone."

Sarah opened the door wider. "Why now?"

Mary stepped inside; her face grim. "Because someone wants to finish what they started."

Chapter Eight: The Reckoning

Mary slipped inside Sarah's house like a shadow, shedding her rain-slick coat and hanging it neatly by the door as if she had all the time in the world. But Sarah could feel it — the urgency in her bones, the ticking of an unseen clock growing louder by the second.

They moved to the kitchen without speaking, the weight of everything unsaid pressing against the silence like a storm about to break.

Sarah offered tea out of habit. Mary declined.

Instead, Mary placed her phone face-down on the table, her eyes never leaving Sarah's.

"I saw the same clip," she said. "But not just that. I've been receiving fragments. Files. Some audio. Some… surveillance. Someone's been collecting on us for a long time."

Sarah nodded, jaw clenched. "Who sent them?"

Mary exhaled slowly. "I don't know. Not yet. But they know what they're doing. They're controlling the narrative. Feeding us just enough to turn us on each other."

Sarah picked up the envelope again — the first one — and laid the photo of Debbie on the table beside it. "She didn't die by accident."

"No." Mary's voice was quiet. "She was executed."

The word sat heavy between them.

"And now someone's putting on a show," Sarah added. "One clip at a time."

Mary leaned forward, her fingers tapping once against the table. "We have to ask the right questions. Not just who's behind this, but why. Why wait until now? Why leak it piece by piece?"

Sarah thought for a moment. "Because they're building something. A spectacle. We're not just witnesses anymore—we're characters. Cast in a play we didn't audition for."

Mary smiled, but there was no joy in it. "Exactly. And we need to figure out who's directing it before the curtain falls."

Silence again, then Sarah whispered, "I think Jane's already broken. She hasn't replied to me in days."

"She's fragile," Mary said, matter-of-fact. "But she won't talk. Not yet. What about Mike?"

Sarah hesitated. "He's unravelling. He was already at his edge. This? This is going to push him over."

Mary's expression darkened. "Then we need to get ahead of this before he does something stupid."

The lights flickered overhead — just for a second — but both women looked up, reflexes on edge.

"Power glitch," Sarah said, trying to sound braver than she felt.

Mary was already pulling a small flash drive from her coat pocket.

"I've downloaded everything I've received so far," she said. "There's more than just the suite footage. They had access to the university servers. Emails. Security feeds. Someone even tapped into our messaging apps."

Sarah's eyes widened. "They've been watching us since before the hotel?"

Mary nodded. "This wasn't just a night that went wrong. It was a setup. And now it's a slow burn. They're seeing who cracks first."

Sarah stood. "We need to find Amy."

Mary's eyes narrowed. "You think she's still alive?"

Sarah's silence was answer enough.

Mary stood too, slipping the flash drive into her coat pocket again.

"Then let's start pulling threads," she said. "And pray the whole thing doesn't unravel before we do."

Mary and Sarah left the house just before dawn. The streets were damp from a light drizzle, and the city was beginning to stir — delivery vans humming past, a jogger in a neon windbreaker slicing through the fog. Normal life moved forward, oblivious to the danger lurking beneath its surface.

They didn't speak much during the drive.

Mary had insisted on taking her car — a low-profile grey saloon with no identifying features. She didn't trust ride shares or taxis. Paranoia? Maybe. But she called it preparation.

They parked in a multi-story garage on the edge of the city. Sarah followed Mary up three flights of stairs to a private office block, most of which was closed or dark this early in the morning.

A security keypad guarded the door at the end of the hall. Mary punched in a code, and the door clicked open.

Inside, the air was stale. A single desk with two chairs. A laptop. A corkboard on the far wall covered in pinned photos, post-it notes, printouts of CCTV stills and messaging app logs — all mapped out in spiderweb lines of red thread.

Sarah stopped just inside the doorway, her eyes widening. "You've been building this for weeks?"

Mary didn't answer right away. She pulled the blinds shut and turned on the desk lamp.

"I started the moment the first clip leaked," she said. "Because I had a feeling it wasn't just an accident. And now you know why."

Sarah moved closer, scanning the board. A name caught her eye — one not part of the group.

"Who's this?" she asked, pointing to a grainy photograph of a man leaning on a motorbike, partially obscured by a hood.

"Unknown," Mary said. "But he's popped up three times — outside the hotel, at the university gate, and just across from Mike's house. Always in the background. Always watching."

Sarah swallowed. "And you think he's our director?"

Mary crossed her arms. "If he's not directing, he's at least holding the camera."

A sharp knock at the office door startled both of them.

Sarah's heart leapt. She reached for the desk instinctively.

Mary raised a hand to silence her, then moved to the door slowly, checking the security cam feed on her phone.

The hallway was empty.

But when she opened the door, a third envelope had been left on the floor.

This one was black.

Mary picked it up carefully, peeled the seal, and inside was a single card — no photos this time.

Just a short line printed in bold serif font:

"You're getting closer. But at what cost?"

She folded the card, slipped it into her coat, and turned back to Sarah.

"Time to escalate."

Chapter Nine: Mike

Mike's knuckles were white around the steering wheel, the hum of his old M-Class Mercedes the only constant as he tore down the country lane. The city lights behind him felt distant, muffled — like another life.

He hadn't slept. Not since the second clip leaked.

It had shown Debbie again. Closer. Slower. The angle was wrong — from above. Not the suite's cameras. A drone?

And then, a frame of Jane. Just her face. Flashing in and out, like an accident or… a warning.

Mike had destroyed his phone an hour ago, slamming it into the kitchen floor until the screen gave way, then dunking the pieces in bleach. But it didn't make him feel safer.

It made him feel watched.

They were all unravelling. And it wasn't just guilt. Someone was orchestrating this. Keeping them paranoid, sleepless, fractured.

And Mike — well, Mike was done waiting.

He pulled off the road and parked at an abandoned quarry he used to visit during his military years, a place no GPS tracked and no signal reached. From the back of the car, he pulled out an old duffle bag — tools, maps, burner phones, and something else he hadn't used since Kandahar.

He dropped the bag at his feet, crouched in the gravel, and took a long breath.

Then he opened the burner phone, dialled a number burned into his memory.

It rang once.

Twice.

Then: "It's been a while."

Mike didn't waste time.

"I need you," he said. "This thing's bigger than I thought."

There was a pause. Then a gravelly voice replied, "You always did pick the complicated ones."

The call ended.

Chapter Ten: The Gathering Storm

Mary sat opposite Sarah in the modest living room of Sarah's rented house, the atmosphere thick with unsaid thoughts. The envelope Sarah had received was now spread open on the coffee table between them like a piece of evidence in an interrogation. The grainy photo. The scrawled message. The image of Debbie, frozen in time.

Mary didn't speak right away. She sipped her lukewarm tea, her eyes drifting to the edges of the room as if half-expecting it to start closing in. Her usually calm demeanour had been slowly unravelling since the second envelope was found.

Sarah broke the silence. "Why me, Mary? Why now?"

Mary blinked, then leaned forward, her fingers steepled in front of her. "Because you're the last neutral party. You weren't in as deep as the others. You kept one foot outside the madness."

Sarah shook her head. "That's not true. I was there. Maybe not the worst of it, but I didn't stop it either."

Mary sighed. "None of us did."

The photograph still sat there, challenging them both. The group had splintered since Debbie's death, paranoia seeping in like damp through old wallpaper. Everyone seemed to suspect everyone else.

Mary reached into her coat pocket and slid something else across the table — a third envelope. "I found this outside my flat last night. Same wax. Same handwriting."

Sarah hesitated, then peeled it open. Inside was no photo this time, but a list of names. Every one of them connected to the group. Her own. Mary's. Mike. Jane. John. Amy. Mark. All neatly typed.

And one more name at the bottom, underlined.

Edward K. Morrison.

Sarah frowned. "Who is this?"

Mary looked grim. "That's what we need to find out."

There was a pause as both women stared at the paper, unease settling over them like fog. Whoever was behind these messages wasn't just playing games anymore — they were orchestrating something much bigger. Something with layers none of them had yet seen.

"Do you think this Morrison is behind it?" Sarah asked.

"I think," Mary said slowly, "he's either behind it — or he's the next target."

Meanwhile, Jane sat alone in a quiet corner of a café across town, a half-drunk latte cooling on the table beside her. Her eyes scanned the article on her phone, the headline blinking in bold:

UNIVERSITY AUTHORITIES ASSIST POLICE IN INVESTIGATION INTO MISSING STUDENT.

A chill crept up her spine. Debbie's name wasn't mentioned, but the timing, the location, the description — it all pointed in one direction. The net was tightening.

She glanced over her shoulder.

Everyone in the café looked normal, indifferent — but then again, so had they once.

Her phone buzzed. A blocked number.

She hesitated, then answered.

A distorted voice crackled on the other end. "You saw the list, didn't you?"

Jane froze. "Who is this?"

"You're being watched. All of you. It's time to choose a side, Jane. Before someone chooses it for you."

The call ended.

Jane sat motionless, heart hammering.

Across the street, in a parked car, a figure watched her through the tinted windshield.

Mike stood, the wind cutting across the quarry floor. He wasn't just preparing anymore. He was going to hunt.

Chapter Eleven: The Watcher

The engine was off, but the car's interior remained warm, humid with the breath of someone who hadn't moved in hours. The figure in the driver's seat sat still, obscured by the tint and a strategically low baseball cap. A long-lens camera rested in the passenger seat, capped for now. The figure's gloved fingers tapped slowly on the steering wheel, rhythmic and patient.

Across the street, Jane still sat in the café. She looked shaken. Good. That was the point.

The figure's phone buzzed — not a call, but a silent notification from a secure messaging app. A single ping.

"She took the call. It's working."

The figure smirked. In the rearview mirror, a second reflection hovered — not a person, but a small red light blinking from the mounted dashcam. It wasn't recording traffic. It was synced with something else.

Fingertips reached for the glove compartment. Inside: a small collection of envelopes, identical to the ones delivered earlier. Red wax seals, crisp parchment, and a printout labelled:

"Phase Two Targets."

The figure rifled past Jane's name, then Sarah's. Then came Mike's.

Next to his name was a symbol. A circle with a horizontal line through it.

Unpredictable. Dangerous. Watch closely.

The figure leaned back, eyes narrowing. Of all the group, Mike was the one most likely to act — not think. He had the military background, the nerves, the tendency to snap. That made him both a threat and a potential tool.

Still watching Jane, the figure spoke softly into a voice recorder:

"Jane responded to prompt. Fear confirmed. Message was received. Subject is now destabilized. Recommend Phase Three to commence by end of week. Further surveillance of Mike begins tonight."

The phone buzzed again. Another message. This one contained a location pin.

"Morrison is moving."

The figure sat up straighter.

Edward K. Morrison. The name at the bottom of the list.

The man no one in the group had ever mentioned aloud — because only a few had ever heard of him. But he knew them. Knew their secrets. Knew Debbie.

Knew the game.

The car started without a sound, electric and near silent. It pulled away from the curb slowly, unnoticed by Jane, who was now paying for her drink with distracted fingers. The figure took one last glance at her through the mirror.

"Your time's coming."

And then the car slipped into the traffic like a phantom, en route to a location only two people in the city even knew existed.

Chapter Twelve: The Rendezvous

The rain began as a whisper against the windshield — fine, misty droplets that blurred the streetlights into long streaks of gold and white. The figure kept the car steady, weaving through the quiet side roads of Nottingham, away from the university, away from the noise. The GPS pinged softly, the blue route line shrinking with every turn. Final destination: a forgotten industrial yard near Colwick, locked behind rusted fences and shrouded by trees that had grown wild from neglect.

The car pulled into the gravel lot, tires crunching beneath. The engine shut off. Silence reclaimed the night.

The figure stepped out, coat drawn tight, head down against the drizzle. The building ahead loomed like a husk — three stories of broken glass and blackened brick. But the rear door had been replaced. Reinforced. There was a keypad beside it, small and new.

A practiced hand entered the code. The lock clicked.

Inside, the air was cooler, drier. The light flickered to life overhead. Just one bulb. Bare. Harsh. A hallway stretched forward, lined with steel doors, numbered but unmarked.

At the end: a door slightly ajar. Through it, a voice.

"You're late."

The figure stepped in. Removed the hat. Droplets slid off the brim. Beneath it, a woman's face — sharp, angular, focused. Her eyes didn't blink as they landed on the man seated behind the desk.

Edward K. Morrison.

He was older than expected. Silver at the
temples. His hands bore the calluses
of someone who'd once worked with
them, but everything else about him
was polished. Sharp suit, a blood-red
tie. A man who once moved in circles
far above academia or underground
orgies. Now? He was the architect of
something more sinister.

"Traffic," she said flatly.

He gestured to the seat across from him. "Sit.
Tell me what you've seen."

She sat. The envelope she carried was
placed on the table between them —
sealed, unopened.

Morrison picked it up and cracked the wax
with a fingernail. Inside: a memory
stick. And a single photo.

Jane. Standing at the café window. Looking
back, as if she sensed someone
watching.

Morrison studied the image and nodded.

"She's folding. Good. And Mike?"

The woman leaned forward. "He's slipping.
Doesn't care anymore. That makes

him the easiest to provoke — or the hardest to control."

Morrison's lips twitched. Not quite a smile. "Both are useful."

He turned to a monitor on the wall and clicked a button. Grainy footage flickered on. The river. The bags. Mike and Mary.

"It's going to unravel," the woman said. "Even Mary's questioning things now."

"That's what we want."

She raised an eyebrow. "And when it does?"

Morrison's gaze was cold.

"Then we start collecting."

He reached into the drawer beside him and pulled out a black folder marked with a gold emblem — the same insignia from the red wax seal.

Inside: files. Photos. Diagrams. Surveillance logs. Debbie's name, circled.

And beneath it, another:

"Target: Sarah."

Chapter Thirteen: A Thread Unravels

Sarah stared at the wall of notes and photographs she'd pinned above her desk — it had started with just the image from the envelope, but now it had grown into something that looked like a conspiracy theorist's fever dream. Strings of red yarn connected blurry surveillance stills, hand-scribbled notes, and maps of Nottingham and Derby. Her once-comfortable flat was now a nest of obsession, lit only by the glow of her laptop and the occasional flicker from the streetlamp outside.

She had spent days combing through every shred of information she could gather. Facial recognition tools. Image metadata. Even amateur forums where true crime fanatics dissected real events like murder mystery novels. And somewhere between the whispers of urban legend and academic scandal, Sarah had found a pattern.

Names. Places. Dead ends.

But something — or someone — connected them all.

She sat cross-legged on her bed, the second envelope Morrison's spy had left still unopened on the bedside table. She had kept it sealed deliberately, fearing what it might confirm. But now… she needed answers. Carefully, she sliced it open with a scalpel from her old med kit.

Inside were three items:

A flash drive.

A folded paper map of Nottingham, circled in three locations: the hotel, the riverbank, and Colwick Industrial Park.

And a third photo. This one made her stomach drop.

It was of her. Alone. Sitting on a park bench. Yesterday.

Someone had been watching her — was still watching her.

She plugged the flash drive into her laptop and clicked open the only file. A video loaded. Grainy, silent surveillance footage. A man and woman entering a building. The timestamp: 2:13 AM. Location: Colwick.

The door behind them had a small keypad.

Sarah's eyes narrowed. The woman's walk — it was familiar. Something in the posture, the tension of her shoulders. She couldn't quite place it.

She scrubbed through the video. A second file auto-played. This time, a voice.

"Mike's slipping... even Mary's questioning things now."

Sarah's blood ran cold.

It was that woman's voice again. Smooth. Controlled.

And then:

"That's what we want."

"Then we start collecting."

She paused the playback and zoomed into the folder Morrison had opened. There — the top page of the dossier.

TARGET: SARAH

She backed away from the desk instinctively, bumping into the chair. They were planning something. She wasn't just a loose end — she was next. The puzzle that had haunted her since Debbie's death now made cruel sense.

This wasn't just about the group anymore. Someone had orchestrated this. Manipulated them. Pushed them toward destruction while recording every move.

The others needed to know. Jane, Mary… even Mike. But who could she trust now?

A noise from the hallway snapped her head around. The floorboard. The third one from the end. It always creaked.

She hadn't moved.

Sarah grabbed the scalpel from her table, her back pressed to the wall as the shadow under her door shifted slightly — pausing.

Someone was outside.

Chapter Fourteen: A Knock at the Edge

Sarah's breath caught in her throat.

The shadow outside the door didn't move again, but the weight of its presence seemed to press against the very air in the flat. She tightened her grip on the scalpel. Her heartbeat pulsed loudly in her ears, every beat a countdown.

She forced herself to breathe slowly. Think. React, don't panic.

The logical part of her brain whispered: Maybe it's just a neighbour. Maybe the floor creaked on its own.

But deep down, she knew better.

Someone was here. Watching. Waiting.

Sarah stepped quietly, barefoot on the wood, slipping across the room toward her wardrobe. She didn't need to open the door to leave — her bedroom window faced the fire escape. If she could just get outside, disappear into the night—

The knock came. Soft. Deliberate.

Not the confused tapping of a delivery driver. No announcement. No voice.

Just that sound.

Three sharp raps.

Sarah froze mid-step.

A moment passed. Then another.

She moved. Fast.

Pulling the wardrobe door wide enough to grab her hoodie, she shrugged it on and reached for the window, unlocking it with a practiced twist. Cold air bit at her cheeks as she slid the pane upward. She swung one leg over the sill and winced at the metal chill of the fire escape beneath her foot.

That's when she heard it.

The click of her front door unlocking.

Someone had a key.

Her heart jumped into her throat as she scrambled through the window, landing harder than she intended on the grating. She kept low, crawling past her bedroom window as she heard the door creak open behind her.

She didn't wait to see who it was.

Down the ladder. One rung at a time. Fast, but silent. She hit the pavement in seconds, eyes flicking across the street. Nothing. No headlights. No movement. The streetlight above her buzzed weakly.

Then a figure appeared in the window — silhouetted. Still. Watching.

They didn't call out. They didn't try to follow.

Sarah didn't stop running.

She didn't go to the university, or Mike's, or even to Jane. Every instinct screamed stay unpredictable.

She ducked into a side alley, heart hammering, breath visible in the chill. Only then did she allow herself to pull out her phone. No signal. She muttered a curse.

But she had the map. She still had the flash drive. And more than anything else — she had the knowledge that someone inside the group was playing a much bigger game.

They all lied. Who will you protect?

That question burned in her mind.

Who had the others sided with? Were they pawns like her, or worse — willing participants?

One thing was certain. She couldn't run forever. She needed to move first. Strike, not hide.

And she knew just the place to start.

Colwick Industrial Park.

Chapter Fifteen: Closing Circles

The morning broke cold and grey over Nottingham. A thin mist hung above the rooftops like something unspoken, suspended in the air. Inside Mike's house, the heavy blinds were drawn, but the atmosphere wasn't hidden — it was tensed, thick with unsaid words and fraying nerves.

Mike sat at the kitchen table; a cup of black coffee untouched in front of him. His fingers drummed an uneven rhythm against the wood grain. Jane paced. Her movements were tight, calculated — not the same woman who had once revelled in danger. Now, there was calculation in her eyes. Survival mode.

"She's gone off the grid," Jane said for the third time, chewing her nail. "No phone. No socials. Nothing. That's not like Sarah."

Mike looked up, eyes shadowed with sleeplessness. "She's smart. Maybe she knows someone's watching."

"She knows more than that," Jane muttered, stopping her pacing. "The envelopes, Mike. That wasn't some prank. That was a message."

He didn't respond. Just stared at the coffee until it cooled. Then, finally, he spoke:

"Mary's not answering either. She left me a voicemail last night. Said something cryptic about debts coming due."

Jane raised an eyebrow. "You think she's talking to the cops?"

"No. Mary wouldn't go to the police." His voice was sure. "But she might be working her own angle."

A knock at the door sliced through the silence.

Jane froze. Mike stood, quietly and quickly moving to the wall to retrieve the Glock he kept behind the framed photo of his Marine unit. He motioned for Jane to stay back and crept toward the door.

He opened it a crack, gun tucked behind his thigh.

No one was there.

Just an envelope on the doorstep.

Red wax. No name.

Jane reached for it before Mike could stop her. She held it up, inspecting the seal.

"A different insignia," she said. "Not the same as Sarah's."

Mike's jaw twitched. "Open it inside."

Back at the table, they peeled it open.

Inside — a USB drive. No note. No threats. Just that.

Mike inserted it into his laptop and let the screen flicker to life. A video file began to play. Low-quality footage, but unmistakable.

It was from that night.

Not the hotel hallway. Not the CCTV from the elevator.

This was inside the room.

The camera was hidden. Possibly inside the bathroom mirror. It showed grainy but clear footage of the group. Of Debbie. Of what followed.

Jane covered her mouth. "Someone's had this… this whole time?"

Mike's fingers curled into fists. "And now they're using it."

He paused the video. On the screen — Mary, stepping forward, saying something to Amy, before turning away. The timestamp put her there minutes before the panic started. Just moments before everything spiralled.

Mike and Jane looked at each other.

"It's not over," she whispered.

"No," Mike said, standing. "It's just beginning."

Chapter Sixteen: Mary in the Silence

Mary had always known how to disappear.

It wasn't a skill learned overnight, but rather over years — long before the incident at the hotel. Before Debbie. Before the envelopes. Before they began to turn on one another like desperate animals in a cage.

She stood now in a disused railway tunnel just outside the Nottingham city limits, the cold biting into her coat. Moss clung to the bricks around her, and overhead, the arching tunnel framed the world like a forgotten entrance to something more ancient than the city above.

A figure approached from the far end, coat long, hood low. Mary didn't flinch. She simply checked her watch. The timing was precise.

"You're late," she said, voice low.

The figure removed their hood — a woman, early forties, sharp eyes. "And you're playing a dangerous game."

Mary nodded once, folding her arms. "Aren't we all?"

The woman handed over a small brown case. Not an envelope. Not a USB stick. This one, something more tangible — papers, files, something old-school. Mary flipped it open briefly, scanning. Her lips tightened. She snapped it shut again.

"You were right," the woman said. "Everything that night — the hotel, the camera, even the original booking — was flagged by someone in internal surveillance. Someone higher than campus security."

Mary's mind raced. "That footage wasn't just being watched... It was being fed somewhere."

The woman nodded grimly. "Whoever's pulling the strings wanted every move documented. From the beginning. And someone in your circle helped them."

Mary took a breath, steadying herself. "Amy?"

"Maybe. Or Mike. Or both. But there's something else."

She hesitated before pulling a second envelope from inside her coat. It was identical to the others, down to the wax seal.

"This one never made it to its intended recipient. It was intercepted. That's why I called you."

Mary opened it slowly.

Inside: a photograph. Sarah — not from the party. But more recently. At a café. Alone. Taken from across the street.

A simple note:

"She's next."

Mary stared at the handwriting. It didn't match the others. This was messier. Almost frantic.

"This isn't just about leverage anymore," Mary whispered. "This is… escalation."

The woman shifted her weight. "You need to decide where your loyalties lie, Mary. Because something much bigger is in play. And this time, it won't be as easy to vanish."

Mary didn't reply. She turned, case in hand, and started back through the tunnel, the cold not bothering her now.

She had questions — too many. But one thing was becoming clear:

Someone had orchestrated the chaos of that night. Someone with reach, with resources, with an eye on them before Debbie's death.

And now, as her former allies scrambled in the dark, Mary knew what she had to do.

Find the origin.

Cut the strings.

And silence the puppeteer.

Chapter Seventeen: Tracing the Source

Mary sat alone in the dim back corner of the university archives room, the overhead light flickering above her as though hesitating to illuminate the truth. Her laptop was open, casting a pale blue glow against her face as her eyes scrolled through files — some official, some not. What she was doing wasn't technically legal, but after everything that had unfolded... she couldn't trust the system to deliver answers.

She hadn't told anyone where she was going. She'd disappeared off the grid for the last few days. No contact with Jane. None with Mike. And definitely not with Sarah. But she hadn't been idle.

It had started with the red seal. That strange insignia stamped into wax — she'd seen it before. Months ago, while reviewing alumni files during an internal audit. A man named Gideon Rourke. He'd donated anonymously, under a shell trust that bore the same symbol — a stylized serpent coiled around a chalice. It was subtle. Intentional.

And now it was showing up again.

She scribbled the name onto the edge of her notebook and drew a line beneath it. Gideon Rourke. The name sounded like something from a novel. But this was no fiction.

Mary leaned back in her chair and cracked her knuckles. She had access to restricted directories through her university credentials — perks of her long career. Rourke had been expelled as a student in the early 2000s. Not for academic misconduct, but for something buried deep: rumours of "unauthorized psychological experiments" during a student retreat. The official report was redacted. He'd vanished shortly after.

She opened the university's hidden archive — a digital cold room, housing reports never meant for daylight — and input a string of search terms. The results were fragmented, but a few threads emerged.

There had been another incident years ago. Another girl. Another cover-up. Same symbol.

Mary swallowed hard. Was this all repeating itself?

Her phone buzzed — not a number she recognized. Just a message:

"He's watching. You're close."

Her blood ran cold.

Someone knew she was digging. But who? And how?

She shut the laptop and gathered her notes, slipping them into her worn leather satchel. She had to move. Not just to stay ahead — but because she now believed something she hadn't allowed herself to accept until this moment:

Debbie's death wasn't an accident.

And worse — the group hadn't been random. They'd been chosen.

Mary exited through the back of the library, the door clicking softly behind her. Outside, the air was thick with mist. Every step felt heavier now, as though the weight of the knowledge she carried slowed her down.

But she wouldn't stop. Not now.

Back in her car, she turned the key and pulled away from the curb. She had one name. One direction.

It was time to find Gideon Rourke.

Chapter Eighteen: The Architect

Mary had always trusted logic. It was her compass in the chaotic seas of human behaviour. But now, that compass spun wildly. The deeper she dug, the less sense the world made — and the more convinced she became that someone had laid the groundwork for this descent long before the first blood was spilled.

The name Gideon Rourke had surfaced like a rotten log breaking the still surface of a black lake — uninvited, ominous, and impossible to ignore.

A man whose name hadn't been spoken around the university in years. Once a prominent psychology professor with a reputation for unconventional — and at times unethical — research into group dynamics, ritual behaviour, and pain thresholds. Dismissed quietly, no charges filed, no official scandal — just vanished into obscurity. But now, his name echoed from the lips of frightened students, whispered in buried campus archives, and found etched into the margins of notebooks that once belonged to Amy.

Mary parked outside the ruins of an old academic retreat centre just north of Derby. It had been shuttered after a fire over a decade ago — supposedly an electrical fault. But the building still stood, half-collapsed and covered in ivy. And someone had been inside recently. The chain on the side gate had been replaced. Fresh cigarette butts lay by the door.

She stepped inside carefully, torchlight sweeping the dust-streaked hallways. Each creak of the floorboards beneath her felt like it could wake the ghosts of the place. But she wasn't here for ghosts. She was here for Gideon.

A faint hum buzzed from deeper inside. Something running. A generator?

Mary followed the sound, descending narrow stairs into the old basement level. Here, the air was cooler, stale, and carried the coppery tang of mildew and decay. Her torch illuminated a door at the end of the corridor. Half open. Beyond it — light.

She eased it open slowly.

Inside was a makeshift office — cables running from a generator in the corner, hooked into old CRT monitors, hard drives, notebooks stacked in towers, and photographs pinned to every wall.

Her stomach dropped.

Photos of the group — from years before. From weeks ago. Some taken in secret. Others from that night. Debbie's face stared back at her in several frames. So did Amy's. Jane's. Her own.

And in the middle of the room sat a man in his sixties, balding, with intense eyes and fingers yellowed from tobacco. He didn't look up when she entered — he was writing in a journal with furious speed.

"Gideon Rourke," she said flatly.

He glanced up, as if mildly inconvenienced.

"You're not supposed to be here," he replied, voice gravelly.

Mary stepped further into the room. "You're the one who started this?"

"No," Gideon said, setting the pen down slowly. "I just opened the door. They walked through it willingly."

"You manipulated them. All of them."

"I showed them who they are beneath the layers of polite society. That was always the goal. To witness the unravelling — the return to instinct."

Mary stared at the wall, at her friends, at the twisted shrine to chaos. "Debbie's dead."

"I know," he said, with no remorse. "I didn't kill her."

"Then who did?"

He shrugged, leaned back in his chair. "Does it matter? She was always going to die. They all are. That's the point."

Mary's hands trembled with rage. "You used us."

"I observed you," he said. "You chose your roles."

She took a step closer. "I'm choosing a new role now."

Gideon smiled. "Are you, Mary? Or are you just another mask, still pretending this isn't exactly what you wanted?"

Behind them, the monitor crackled. A new image blinked onto the screen — someone else watching. Not Gideon. A third party.

Mary turned sharply.

"Who's that?" she asked.

Gideon didn't reply. His face had finally changed — the smug confidence replaced by something that looked like fear.

Mary felt her blood chill.

They weren't alone in the game.

They never had been.

Chapter Nineteen: The Tipping Point

Sarah stood on the rooftop of the campus library, wind tangling her hair as she stared across the sea of buildings cloaked in late-night mist. The envelope from earlier still burned in her jacket pocket like a brand. She hadn't shown Jane everything. Not yet. Not until she could confirm what she feared.

Because one of the photos in the envelope hadn't been taken on the night Debbie died — it had been taken the day before. In it, Sarah was walking alongside Amy in Derby. A moment she didn't remember, wearing clothes she didn't recognize, her own face partially turned away.

A fabricated image?

Or something much worse?

She'd started doubting herself. Her memory. The timeline. And now, with Jane growing more distant and Mary completely off the grid, the only person she could trust was herself — and that felt increasingly dangerous.

The campus below was quiet. Too quiet. She knew the police were circling. Detectives had been to her flat twice now, asking about Amy, about Debbie. They had that look — like they already knew more than they were saying. Like they were waiting for her to slip.

But what if someone wanted her to?

Sarah had begun noticing things: shadows moving where no one should be, people watching her from cars parked too long outside her building, messages erased from her phone, emails she didn't remember writing. Paranoia was no longer just a possibility — it was survival instinct.

She stepped back from the edge, phone clutched in her hand, the screen glowing with the name of a secure contact: A. F. — someone Amy had once trusted, someone who'd helped her with past... projects.

With trembling fingers, Sarah tapped a message:

"I think we were part of something bigger. I need to know what Amy knew. Before she disappeared. Before Debbie died."

She hit send.

A response came almost instantly:

"Meet me. Tonight. You're already being watched."

Her blood ran cold.

She spun, suddenly hyper-aware of the open rooftop. But no one was there.

She took the stairs down two at a time, exiting through a side door and into the chilled air of the car park, where only a few lights flickered against the fog.

That's when she saw it — a figure across the lot, leaning against a lamppost, hood up, unmoving Not Gideon. Not Mike.

Someone else.

They didn't approach.

But they were waiting.

Sarah didn't move either. Her instincts screamed to run, but something deeper kept her rooted. Because for all the fear, there was a pull to this moment — a strange gravity, like finally stepping into the frame of a painting she'd spent weeks circling.

Her phone buzzed again.

"You're close. Just follow the lights."

The lamppost nearest the figure flickered. Then the next. A path illuminating toward a side gate near the edge of campus.

Sarah took one step. Then another.

She didn't know who was leading her anymore — but she knew she couldn't turn back.

As she passed the figure by the lamppost, they didn't speak, didn't even lift their head.

But she could feel it.

They knew her name.

And they knew exactly what she'd done.

Chapter Twenty: The Circle Narrows

Sarah's footsteps echoed softly against the cold, tiled corridor beneath the abandoned wing of the university. She'd followed the instructions from the latest message—no phone, no bag, just the note tucked inside her coat lining and the steady thrum of adrenaline. The hallway smelled of old bleach and damp stone, a forgotten artery of the building she'd passed a hundred times but never truly noticed.

A security door stood at the far end, slightly ajar, its keypad blinking amber. No code needed. Someone wanted her inside.

She hesitated. Her reflection in the dusty glass showed more than tiredness. She looked hunted. Her eyes, once sharp with clinical precision, now flickered with uncertainty.

A voice called from within. Male. Calm.

"Come on, Sarah. You're late."

She stepped through.

The room was dim, lit only by a cluster of overhead projectors casting old photographs onto whitewashed brick walls. The images shifted every few seconds—shots from hotel corridors, CCTV captures, blurred faces laughing, crying, recoiling. Her own face appeared. Mark's. Mary's. Jane's. Mike's. Debbie's.

At a long table, a man stood with his back to her. His silhouette was tall, deliberate. He was placing papers into a leather-bound folder, methodically.

"Who are you?" she asked, her voice low, wary.

He turned. Not young, but not old—somewhere in that ambiguous middle, with sharp eyes that didn't miss a flicker of movement. His voice was calm and practiced, like someone who'd delivered too many bad truths in rooms like this.

"My name is Morrison. I'm not the one pulling strings. I'm just the one who still knows how to tie them."

Sarah didn't move. "You've been watching us."

"For a long time."

"Why?"

"Because one of you was never supposed to survive that night." He met her gaze. "And now someone wants to finish what they started."

Sarah's pulse surged. "Debbie?"

He nodded. "And not just her."

The projectors clicked to another image—this one recent. A man in a car. Another of Amy, in a disguise she thought had fooled everyone. A third image—Sarah herself, entering this very building just ten minutes ago.

Sarah's breath hitched. "Are you the one sending the envelopes?"

"No. But I've intercepted a few. Enough to know you're not safe, and neither is anyone else connected to that night."

He slid a file across the table. "Inside, you'll find names. Accounts. Surveillance logs. Even connections to someone higher—someone no one in your group knows is involved. Yet."

Sarah opened the folder slowly. The first name nearly made her knees give out.

Mary Winton.

Morrison watched her reaction with a grim satisfaction.

"She's not who you think she is."

Sarah looked up. "And what do you want from me?"

He leaned forward. "Help me stop what's coming next. Because if we don't, this won't be about a single body in a river or a cover-up. This will spiral into something far worse. And you'll all be at the centre of it."

She stared at the names, the evidence, the photos. Her hands closed around the folder.

"Then let's begin."

Chapter Twenty-One: The Marionette's Hand

Mary's breath hung in the cool, dry air of the subterranean chamber beneath the chapel ruins outside Nottingham. She moved like a ghost through the underground catacombs, each footstep echoing against walls that hadn't heard a voice in years — at least not one that didn't whisper secrets.

She held the flashlight low, the beam skimming across dusty floors and the cracked remains of mosaic tiles. Her phone had no signal. She wasn't surprised. This place wasn't on any map.

Ahead, a heavy iron gate groaned open before she could reach it.

"Mary," said the voice. Soft. Male. Elegant. Like silk draped over a knife.

He was waiting.

Gideon Rourke.

She had pieced the name together from fragments—old university grants, shell charities, obscure footnotes in funding records for experimental psychological studies. She traced the financial shadows from Amy's application all the way back to a defunct think tank connected to an elite network once exposed in a brief investigative report. The reporter vanished before publishing part two.

Mary stepped forward into the light of the chamber.

Rourke stood with perfect posture, tall and precise, in a tailored coat. His hair was silver at the temples, and his smile didn't reach his eyes.

"You've come far," he said.

"I had help," Mary replied, calm but alert.

He gestured to the circle of books, scrolls, and old reels of film that surrounded the room's centrepiece — a low table bearing the red wax insignia she'd seen too many times to ignore.

"The others think they were playing a game of guilt and secrets," Rourke said. "They don't understand they were being played."

Mary stayed silent.

He stepped closer. "But you—you knew there was something more. A reason each member of the group was chosen. That night wasn't an accident, Mary. Debbie's death wasn't collateral damage. It was a test."

Mary stiffened. "A test?"

Rourke's smile curved, serpent-like.

"Your reactions. Your loyalties. Your fears. We placed each of you into that room not for what you'd done—but what you might do, when pushed far enough."

Mary's voice was steel. "Why?"

"Because we're preparing for something bigger. And people like you—smart, adaptable, willing to lie, to cut— you're candidates."

Mary's heartbeat faster, but she kept her face still.

"And Debbie?" she asked. "Was she a candidate too?"

"She was the spark," Rourke said. "But she was never meant to survive. You were always meant to choose."

Mary looked down at the red wax symbols scrawled in patterns across the table — not just sigils, but coordinates. Locations. Dates.

"What are you planning?"

Rourke leaned in, his voice now a whisper.

"Awakening."

The lights flickered, as if the chamber itself trembled at the word. Mary's jaw clenched.

"You'll never get them all to join you," she said.

Rourke's expression didn't change.

"They already have."

From behind her, a second set of footsteps approached.

Mary turned. Mike stood in the doorway, his face unreadable.

"Hello, Mary," he said quietly.

Mary's eyes widened — not in shock, but confirmation

She had feared this moment.

Now it was here.

Chapter Twenty-Two: Bloodlines and Blind Faith

Mary didn't move. The air between her and Mike was colder than the stone beneath their feet. The low flicker of candlelight painted shadows across his face — shadows she hadn't seen in him before.

"How long have you known?" she asked, keeping her voice steady.

Mike didn't answer right away. His eyes, once hard with instinctive defense, now brimmed with something else. Not remorse. Not pride. Resignation.

"Long enough," he finally said. "Long enough to stop asking questions."

Rourke watched them both from behind his steepled fingers. "He was one of the first. Recruited for his loyalty. For his... adaptability."

Mary's lip curled. "You used us. All of us."

"No," Rourke said gently. "We gave you an opportunity. The world you thought you lived in? A fabrication. A surface-level distraction. We pulled back the curtain."

"You killed an innocent girl," Mary snapped. "You called it a test."

Rourke leaned forward. "And you passed it, Mary. Don't forget that."

Mike took a step closer, voice low. "You think I wanted it to go that far? That any of us did?" His jaw flexed. "But once it started, it couldn't stop. We couldn't stop."

She looked at him, searching his face. "So what now, Mike? You hand me over too? Offer me up as proof of your loyalty?"

He shook his head. "No. I brought you here so you could see it for yourself. The truth. Everything you thought you understood — the university, the grants, the research — it was all the first layer. The real program runs deeper."

Mary's fists clenched at her sides.

"The others — Jane, Sarah, even Amy — they've seen flashes of it," Mike said. "But you've seen the shape of it. You're closer than any of them."

Rourke stood slowly, the chamber darkening behind him. "We can offer you a place at the table. All the questions that keep you awake at night? We can answer them. But you must let go of what you think justice looks like."

Mary's heartbeat thundered in her ears.

"You're offering me power," she said. "At the cost of my soul."

Mike looked away.

Rourke smiled thinly. "You'd be surprised how quickly ideals fade when the alternative is irrelevance."

Silence hung, thick and weighted.

Then Mary stepped forward. "Show me. Everything."

Mike blinked. "What?"

"I want to know what you've been hiding," she said. "But don't mistake this for loyalty. I'm not here to join your cult. I'm here to understand it."

Rourke chuckled. "Curiosity. The first step to conversion."

Mary turned to him. "It's the first step to exposure."

The tension cracked, electric.

Mike opened a steel door embedded in the stone. A faint hum echoed from within — something mechanical, something alive. Mary followed, her steps sure.

Behind them, Rourke whispered into the shadows. "She's the one. Watch her."

A figure moved in the dark.

The puppet master's grip tightened.

Chapter Twenty-Three: The Vault Beneath

The heavy steel door groaned as Mike pushed it open, the thick scent of ozone hitting Mary's senses immediately. The chamber beyond was unlike anything she had expected.

Rows of servers lined the walls, cables snaking along the floor like veins. Low, pulsing blue lights illuminated a central structure — a glass-walled vault suspended in the centre of the room by thick steel chains. Inside the vault, something glowed faintly, a steady rhythmic pulse, almost like a heartbeat.

"What is this?" Mary whispered, stepping over the threshold.

Mike didn't answer immediately. He motioned for her to follow him across the narrow catwalk leading to the central platform. Their footsteps echoed, hollow and eerie.

"This," Mike said at last, his voice carrying a strange mixture of awe and regret, "is what they've been building for years. Data. DNA. Surveillance. They've been collecting everything. Not just from us — from the entire city. The university was just a front."

Mary frowned, feeling the chill seep deeper into her bones. "Collecting for what?"

Rourke's voice drifted in from behind them. "Prediction. Control. Evolution."

Mary turned to face him. His silhouette loomed in the doorway, calm and unhurried.

"You think wars are fought with guns now?" Rourke said, stepping onto the catwalk. "No. The real wars are fought here. Control information, control the future. Control the bloodline, control destiny."

Mary swallowed hard. Her mind raced. This wasn't just about a sadistic group covering their tracks — it was about something far larger. They had plans for them. They had plans for everyone.

Inside the glass vault, Mary could now see objects pinned like grotesque trophies — blood samples, personal effects, even fragments of memories. Tiny flashes of faces, voices, moments — all captured, digitized, and archived.

Debbie's locket glinted from one corner.

She stepped closer, her fists tightening. "You're building a weapon," she said. "One made of flesh and secrets."

Mike looked down. "They call it The Mosaic. Piece by piece, creating something... unstoppable."

"And what about us?" Mary asked. "Were we just experiments too?"

Rourke's smile was almost tender. "You were catalysts. Test subjects. Proof of concept."

Mary's jaw set hard. "You underestimated us."

Rourke raised an eyebrow. "Did we?"

For a beat, the only sound was the hum of the vault and the distant clicking of cooling fans.

Mary turned to Mike, voice low and urgent. "We have to destroy it."

Mike's expression flickered — fear, doubt, hope — all warring beneath the surface. "It's not that simple.

"It never is," she said. "But we have to."

From the corner of her eye, Mary spotted movement in the vault — a shadow. A flicker of something alive. She stiffened.

Rourke saw her look. "You're not the first to want to bring it all down," he said. "And you won't be the last."

Mary squared her shoulders. "Maybe not. But I'll be the one who succeeds."

The overhead lights flickered. Somewhere deep below them, a siren began to whine — a low, mournful sound like the world itself crying out.

Mike stepped forward, determination sharpening his features. "Tell me what to do."

Mary met his eyes. No more half-measures. No more fear.

"We take the whole system offline," she said. "Tonight."

Behind them, unseen in the darkness, the puppet master leaned forward, watching.

Smiling.

Chapter Twenty-Four: Sabotage

Mary moved with urgency, her boots slamming across the catwalk as she surveyed the vault's inner workings. Everything depended on speed. Rourke might have let them glimpse the truth, but he wasn't about to stand back and watch them destroy it.

Mike peeled open a panel along the wall, revealing a tangle of coloured wires and glowing circuit boards. "Overload the server's coolant systems," he muttered, yanking a multi-tool from his belt. "It'll fry the processors and cause a chain reaction."

"How long do we have once it starts?" Mary asked, already scanning the room for other vulnerabilities.

"Ten minutes tops before it blows. Less if the failsafe's kick in."

Mary nodded grimly. That was enough. It had to be.

Behind them, Rourke watched with maddening calm, as if he were observing a play he had written long ago. "You really think collapsing this little node will stop the greater machine?" he said, voice almost soft.

"No," Mary said without looking back. "But it'll send a message."

Rourke chuckled under his breath. "Messages are for the living."

Mike didn't answer — he was working too fast now, sweat starting to bead on his forehead.

Mary dashed toward the nearest control station, scanning the readouts. She caught sight of a master override code blinking in red — an emergency shutdown sequence that could be manually triggered if they cut the right circuit.

She shouted over her shoulder, "I need you to kill the primary security feed! Now!"

Mike cursed under his breath but obeyed, sparking a blade across the wiring.

Sparks showered down as a screen flickered and went dead.

Immediately, the room dimmed.

The heartbeat-like pulse inside the vault stuttered.

Mary felt the air shift — like the vault was waking up.

"No turning back now," Mike muttered.

The sirens intensified. From deeper within the complex, Mary heard the pounding of boots — reinforcements on their way. The organization wasn't going to let this go without a fight.

Rourke stepped forward, hands up. "Stop this madness," he said. "You don't know what you're doing. You're ripping apart the future!"

Mary stared at him, feeling the fury rise in her chest. "The future isn't yours to control."

She turned back to Mike. "Hit the coolant lines now!"

Mike jammed the blade into a coolant mainframe. Instantly, a high-pressure hiss filled the room as supercooled vapor burst into the air.

The vault's glass began to crack, spiderwebbing fractures shooting outward. The glowing objects inside the chamber flickered, like dying stars.

Sirens, shouting, the creak of collapsing machinery — the chamber was turning into chaos Mike grabbed Mary's arm. "Time to go!"

As they ran back across the catwalk, a deafening rumble shook the room. The servers along the walls began exploding one by one, bursts of fire and sparks lighting up the darkness.

Behind them, Rourke stood motionless, watching it burn, a strange smile on his lips.

Almost... proud.

Mary and Mike burst into the stairwell as the first explosions rocked the chamber.

Concrete dust filled the air. Pipes burst. Alarms screamed.

They didn't look back.

At the top of the stairs, they stumbled into a narrow service corridor lit by flickering emergency lights. Mary's chest burned, but she forced herself forward.

"Where's the exit?" Mike shouted over the din.

"This way!" Mary yelled, dragging him toward a hatch door labelled 'Maintenance - Surface Access.'

She spun the wheel. The door groaned, stuck.

Mike slammed his shoulder against it. Once, twice.

It popped open with a shriek.

Cold night air rushed over them like a blessing.

They emerged into the dark, deserted woods behind the university's industrial labs. Stars wheeled overhead in a black sky. Somewhere far behind them, the ground shuddered again — a muted whump as the chamber collapsed into itself.

Mike bent over, gasping for breath, his face streaked with grime.

Mary stood tall, her heart still pounding. She stared back toward the faint glow of the fires.

It was done.

At least... for now.

Mike wiped his mouth with the back of his hand. "You think we bought ourselves any time?"

Mary shook her head, solemn. "No. We just moved up their list."

From the shadows, another figure watched them.

A different puppet master.

And the real game was only just beginning.

Chapter Twenty-Five: Ghosts Rising

Smoke curled above the treetops, drifting toward the cold stars.

Sarah watched from the crest of a nearby hill, her breath steaming in the night air.

She had seen the explosions light up the forest floor like a heartbeat, one blast after another until the ground seemed to ripple. She hadn't been close enough to be caught, but she had been close enough to understand.

Mike and Mary had pulled the trigger.

She should have felt relief — a twisted, vengeful satisfaction at the thought of Rourke's secret empire burning to the ground. But instead, a sick knot tightened in her gut.

The burning vault hadn't ended anything.

It had started something much worse.

Her phone buzzed quietly against her thigh.

A message. Unknown number.

"New players inbound. Watch your back. -G"

Gideon Rourke.

Still alive.

Still moving his pieces.

Sarah swore under her breath and pocketed the phone. She pulled her jacket tighter around herself and started down the hill toward the city lights.

Somewhere, someone was filling the vacuum the Blood Spurts had left behind.

Someone worse.

Across the city, deep underground, the puppet master moved quietly through an old service tunnel that hadn't seen maintenance in decades. A black-gloved hand slid across a sealed steel hatch, tapping a code into a recessed keypad.

The door hissed open.

Inside, a new nerve centre buzzed to life — fresh servers, fresh personnel. Men and women in dark clothes moved with clinical precision, ready to pick up where Rourke had fallen.

The puppet master — not Rourke, but someone Rourke had only ever feared from afar — smiled beneath their mask.

"Phase Two is green-lit," they said into a headset.

A voice crackled back: "Targets?"

"Primary: Blood Spurts survivors.

Secondary: University and city infrastructure.

Tertiary: All liabilities."

The puppet master's hand hovered briefly over a series of live feeds — blurry surveillance footage of Mike, Mary, Jane, and Sarah moving separately through the night.

Then the hand closed into a fist.

"No loose ends."

Mike and Mary stumbled across the frost-rimmed parking lot behind the industrial labs, still running on adrenaline and sheer stubbornness. Every muscle in Mike's body screamed for rest, but he knew better.

They were still in the crosshairs.

"We need a new plan," Mary gasped.

Mike shook his head. "No. We need to disappear."

Mary shot him a look — fierce, almost wild. "Disappear? After everything we've learned? After what they did to Debbie?"

Mike closed his eyes for a second, the weight of it all crushing him.

"I'm not talking about surrender," he said finally. "I'm talking about war."

Mary's lips curved into a cold, dangerous smile. "Good."

The faint howl of sirens echoed across the distant streets.

They needed allies. Resources. Time.

They had none.

But they still had one advantage:

They knew the truth now.

And maybe — just maybe — they could weaponize it.

Sarah ducked into a side street, instincts prickling.

Someone was following her.

Not Rourke's old goons. These steps were too careful. Too quiet.

Professional.

She slipped her hand into her pocket, wrapping her fingers around the cold metal of the tiny switchblade she had carried since the night Debbie died.

Not today, she thought grimly.

Not without a fight.

Back at the ruins of the vault, fire crews battled the flames.

A man in a clean black suit stood on a nearby ridge, watching.

He adjusted his cufflinks, speaking into a hidden mic.

"Subject Zero has been terminated," he said calmly. "Proceeding to secondary acquisitions."

Far beneath his feet, something stirred in the wreckage — not dead, but waiting.

The Blood Spurts thought they had burned the sickness out of the system.

But all they had done was light a fuse.

And the real explosion was still to come.

Chapter Twenty-Six: Hunters and Hunted

The night bled into early morning; the cold biting deeper as Sarah kept moving.

Every shadow seemed alive now. Every silence loaded with unseen threats.

Down the alley. Across the desolate park.

No place felt safe anymore.

She needed to find Mike and Mary — she needed to regroup before she was picked off like an easy target.

But even as she thought it, Sarah knew: the old alliances were shattered. Trust was a dying currency.

Her phone buzzed again. Another unknown number.

"Corner of Wilton and 8th. 10 minutes. Come alone."

A shiver passed through her. No name, no reassurance.

But something inside her — the same stubborn core that had survived everything so far — clicked into place.

She wasn't going to run anymore.

Tucking the blade tighter into her sleeve, Sarah disappeared into the waking city.

Mike crouched beside a battered black SUV, breathing hard, eyes scanning the horizon.

Mary stood behind him, arms crossed, jacket torn and streaked with dirt.

"Something's wrong," she muttered, checking her battered burner phone for the tenth time. "Sarah should've called back by now."

Mike wiped a smear of blood from his forehead. "Sarah's smart. If she's silent, it's because she's trying to stay alive."

Mary nodded grimly but didn't look convinced.

Far off, a siren wailed — not police, but something worse.

Private security. Hired guns.

Mike leaned closer; voice low: "We stick to the plan. Meet at the fallback spot if we get separated. No heroics."

Mary gave a bitter laugh. "We stopped being heroes the night Debbie died."

Mike didn't argue. He just tightened the straps on the stolen backpack — cash, burner phones, forged IDs — everything they needed to vanish if the worst came

"Ready?" he asked.

Mary smiled a humourless smile. "Born ready."

They slipped into the misty streets like wraiths, hunted and hunting all at once.

Sarah's boots crunched against broken glass as she approached the meeting point.

Wilton and 8th — a half-abandoned industrial zone, grim and silent.

A flicker of movement ahead caught her eye — a figure, hooded, standing perfectly still beneath a flickering streetlamp.

No backup. No obvious weapon.

Sarah didn't hesitate. She moved forward, knife ready, heart thundering.

"Sarah," the figure said — low, female, almost familiar.

Jane.

Sarah blinked, thrown off for a split second.

"What the hell are you doing here?" she demanded.

Jane's face was pale, eyes hollowed out with exhaustion. "Same as you. Trying to survive."

"That message — was it you?"

Jane shook her head. "No. Someone else set this up. They want us in the open. Vulnerable."

Sarah's stomach twisted.

A sharp crack rang out — the unmistakable sound of a suppressed gunshot.

Both women ducked instinctively, sprinting toward the shattered remains of a warehouse across the street.

Inside, darkness swallowed them.

Sarah's mind raced:

Who else knew they'd be here?

And why hadn't Jane warned her sooner?

In the control van a block away, the new player — the one who had inherited Rourke's scattered empire — leaned over the monitor bank, watching the feeds.

"Target One and Target Three in play," an operative reported.

"Hold fire," the leader said. "Let them sweat."

Another operative hesitated. "Orders on the man and woman at perimeter?"

The leader smiled coldly.

"Capture alive if possible. But if they fight..."

A casual shrug.

"End them."

The Blood Spurts survivors were valuable. Their suffering, even more so.

Mary pressed herself against the SUV's frame, one hand on Mike's arm, freezing him mid-step.

"You hear that?" she whispered.

Mike tilted his head.

Helicopter blades. Distant, but closing fast.

"We need to move," he growled.

But before they could retreat, headlights slashed through the darkness — three black SUVs fanning out across the abandoned lot.

Doors opened. Men in tactical gear spilled out, weapons raised.

Mary's mouth went dry.

Mike gave her one hard look.

"No surrender," he said.

Mary nodded grimly. "No mercy. Together, they dove into the shadows, hunted animals fighting for their lives.

Sarah and Jane crashed through the warehouse's rotting side door, lungs burning.

They stumbled into a cavernous space filled with ancient machinery, rusted beams, and shattered glass.

Jane gasped, pointing: "There! A service hatch!"

They ran — just as more gunfire shredded the air around them.

Sarah slammed her shoulder against the hatch. It groaned open, revealing a narrow staircase spiralling down into darkness.

Without hesitation, they plunged into the depths.

Above them, heavy boots pounded closer.

Sarah didn't look back. She just kept moving, deeper and deeper, into the guts of the city — hoping that somewhere ahead, there was a way out.

Chapter Twenty-Seven: Into the Dark

The staircase twisted downward into pure blackness, the air growing colder, damper, heavier with every step.

Sarah's heart hammered in her chest. Each breath felt like dragging ice into her lungs.

Jane stumbled behind her, one hand gripping the back of Sarah's jacket to stay upright in the darkness.

Somewhere above, they heard boots striking concrete.

The hunters weren't giving up.

Sarah reached the bottom first, groping for a wall, a door, anything. Her fingers brushed cold steel — an industrial access door, battered but still solid.

"Help me!" she hissed.

Together, she and Jane forced their weight against it. It groaned, then snapped open with a violent screech, spilling them into another underground tunnel — this one even older, crumbling with age.

Old maintenance lines, Sarah guessed. Forgotten by the city. Perfect for disappearing — or dying.

"We have to keep moving," she whispered, pulling Jane forward.

They didn't dare use a light. They stumbled through the dark, following the stale breath of air that hinted at another way out.

Behind them, the thudding boots paused. Voices murmured. Orders were given.

Sarah knew what came next — they'd send trackers. Dogs maybe. Heat sensors.

We're running out of time.

Across the city, Mike and Mary fought their own desperate battle.

Mike led them through the twisted alleys, ducking between broken fences and abandoned shops. He kept his head low, movements quick and sharp. Mary matched him stride for stride, gun drawn from the stash Mike had kept hidden under the SUV's seat.

"They're herding us," Mike said between breaths. "They want us boxed in."

"Good luck with that," Mary muttered.

Ahead, the way narrowed — a dead-end alley.

Mike swore under his breath.

From the rooftops, a laser sight danced briefly across Mary's shoulder. She ducked instinctively, firing a shot upward without hesitation.

Glass shattered.

A cry of pain.

"Down!" Mike barked, dragging her into a side door half hanging off its hinges.

Inside, they found a maze of back corridors, once offices, now just hollowed-out husks.

"We can still make it," Mike said, voice low and tight. "Get to the fallback."

Mary nodded grimly. "And if we can't?"

Mike gave a brutal grin.

"Then we take as many of them with us as we can."

Underground, Sarah stumbled over a fallen pipe, catching herself just before she hit the floor.

She realized suddenly that Jane wasn't behind her anymore.

"Jane?" she hissed, turning back.

Silence.

"Jane!"

A faint scuffing noise. Sarah spun — and saw Jane slumped against the tunnel wall, clutching her side, blood seeping through her fingers.

"No, no, no," Sarah muttered, rushing back.

"I'm fine," Jane gasped. "Keep going."

"Like hell," Sarah snapped. "Come on."

She hoisted Jane's arm over her shoulder. Jane was weaker than she let on, every step slower. But they moved.

They had to.

At the far end of the tunnel, a faint light glowed.

An exit?

Or another trap?

Sarah didn't care anymore. She just knew they couldn't stay here.

The figure in the control van — the one orchestrating the night's hunt — watched the monitors with clinical detachment.

"They're splitting up," the tech murmured. "Standard survival pattern."

"Predictable," the leader said, leaning back, fingers steepled.

"Let them run a little longer. The deeper the fear, the sweeter the fall."

Mike and Mary burst into a wider street — briefly illuminated by flickering neon from a boarded-up diner.

The SUVs were nowhere in sight.

For now.

Mike checked his watch.

Five minutes until the rendezvous time with Sarah — if she made it.

"You trust her?" Mary asked, reading his mind.

Mike didn't hesitate. "With my life."

Mary gave a grim little smile. "Then let's go earn that trust."

They took off again, disappearing into the maze of a city that no longer belonged to them.

Sarah and Jane finally staggered into a maintenance shaft — a battered ladder leading up toward a manhole cover faintly outlined by streetlight above.

"Freedom," Sarah whispered hoarsely.

A shout echoed behind them.

The hunters were coming.

Jane started to climb. Sarah followed, heart pounding in her throat.

Halfway up, a shot rang out — sparking off the ladder, inches from Sarah's foot.

Another. Closer.

Sarah didn't look back.

She just climbed faster, muscles screaming, every instinct yelling at her to survive.

Jane reached the top, pushed against the manhole — and it gave way.

Fresh, freezing air rushed in.

They tumbled out into a side street — cracked pavement, broken streetlights.

No time to rest.

No time to think.

Sarah dragged Jane to her feet.

From the shadows ahead, she saw a figure moving — fast, purposeful.

Mike.

And Mary.

Relief flooded Sarah so hard she almost dropped Jane.

Mike skidded to a halt when he saw them, shock flashing across his face.

"Come on!" he barked, waving them forward.

Behind them, more figures spilled from the tunnels, dark shapes, weapons glinting under the sickly streetlights.

No time left.

Together, the battered survivors ran — into the heart of the city's ruins, into the jaws of whatever came next.

Hunters. Hunted.

No more difference between them now.

Only who could outlast the night.

Chapter Twenty-Eight: No More Running

The city around them was a skeleton, hollowed and broken, the streets cracked and empty.

Mike led the group, weaving through alleyways and crumbling industrial lots, one hand steadying Sarah as she half-carried Jane along.

Behind them, the hunters moved like shadows, always just out of sight — but never far enough.

Mike pulled them into the shell of an old textile factory. Huge iron beams loomed overhead, the roof sagging and riddled with holes where moonlight poured through in thin silver streams. Dust danced like spectres in the light.

They crouched behind a rusted loom, catching their breath.

Jane slumped to the ground, blood staining her side. She was fading fast, every breath a shallow rasp.

"We can't keep running," Sarah said, wiping sweat from her forehead. Her voice was low, furious. "They'll pick us off."

Mike nodded grimly. "Then we stop running."

He rose to his feet, drawing a heavy black pistol from inside his jacket — the last of his personal arsenal.

"If they want a war," he said, voice steady and cold, "we'll give them one."

Mary, leaning against a cracked pillar, cracked a grin despite the bruises mottling her face.

"About time," she said.

Sarah hesitated.

Fighting meant killing. Fighting meant losing any chance of slipping away quietly.

But looking at Jane — looking at all they'd lost already — she realized they were past that now.

She stood. "I'm in."

Mike glanced at her, approval flickering briefly in his hardened eyes.

"Good. Because here they come."

Footsteps.

Lots of them.

The hunters moved into the factory with calculated precision, spreading out, weapons raised.

A voice boomed from the shadows — amplified by a handheld speaker.

"Give up. There's nowhere left to run."

Mike stepped into the open, his silhouette framed by the broken windows and the sickly city lights beyond.

"You first," he called back, raising his weapon.

The hunters hesitated.

Just for a second.

And that second was all Mike needed.

The first shot echoed like a thunderclap through the dead city.

One of the hunters dropped, weapon clattering from his hand.

Chaos erupted.

Mary rolled into cover, firing short, disciplined bursts. Sarah grabbed a metal rod from the floor and smashed the nearest attacker's knee, sending him sprawling. Mike moved like a machine, his shots brutal and precise, forcing the hunters back step by step.

But it wasn't enough.

They were too many.

From a high catwalk above, a shadow moved — different from the others. Not just another mercenary. Something else.

A sharp voice cut through the gunfire.

"Enough!"

The hunters froze instantly, weapons dropping to low ready.

From the shadows stepped a man in a dark coat — face hidden under a pulled-down cap.

Sarah recognized him immediately.

Gideon Rourke.

The true hand behind the Blood Spurts chaos.

The spider at the centre of the web.

"You don't understand what you've stumbled into," Gideon said, voice smooth as oil.

Mike didn't lower his gun.

"Try me."

Gideon smiled — a slow, sad thing.

"You think you're fighting for survival. But you've already lost. This was never about you. Not really. You're pieces on a board you can't even see."

Mary stepped forward, weapon steady.

"What do you want?"

Gideon's eyes glittered in the half-light.

"Truth," he said.

"And blood. Always blood."

From the rafters, more shadows gathered — not mercenaries.

Other survivors. Other victims.

Faces they recognized: people from the University. From the streets.

Recruits.

Slaves.

Followers.

The Blood Spurts had grown far beyond a twisted game.

It was a movement now.

And they were caught in its storm.

Mike realized it then, deep in his bones:

There was no winning.

Only surviving.

Only burning it all down.

He turned to Mary, to Sarah, even to the barely-conscious Jane.

"One last stand," he said quietly.

"Or we die on our knees."

Mary raised her pistol. Sarah gripped the metal rod tighter.

Jane, pale but conscious, nodded weakly.

They were bloodied.

They were broken.

But they weren't finished.

Not yet.

Mike smiled grimly at Gideon Rourke — and opened fire.

Chapter 29: The Circle Narrows

The flickering light above them buzzed with static as Mike leaned against the cold wall of the chamber, eyes locked on Mary. Her expression was unreadable, yet her fingers tightened around the worn edge of the folder she'd recovered from Gideon's vault.

She had opened it only moments before, but her silence since had been louder than any scream.

"You're going to have to say something," Mike said, voice low, the tension between them thick enough to choke on. "I've seen men freeze up under fire, Mary. But this?"

She turned the folder slowly toward him, and his eyes scanned the pages: surveillance photos, transcripts, university documents... and a list. Seven names. One of them crossed out in red: Debbie Holloway.

Mike's jaw clenched. "They were targeting us?"

Mary nodded. "Not just us. The society existed long before we stumbled into it. But someone started watching — cataloguing our behaviour. This isn't just about Debbie. This is about leverage. Control."

Mike stepped back, the walls of the chamber seeming to close in tighter. "And Gideon?"

"He's not the architect. He's an archivist," she said bitterly. "Someone else is pulling the strings. This—" she tapped the list, "—was a grooming operation. Psychological experimentation wrapped in pleasure, wrapped in secrecy."

Mike ran a hand through his hair. "So who's the real target?"

Mary looked up at him, her voice sharp. "All of us."

A door creaked somewhere behind them — not the main one they entered through.

Both froze.

Footsteps echoed down a hallway they hadn't seen before, concealed behind a panel Gideon had never mentioned. A new voice floated through the dark, precise and cold.

"You were never meant to come this far."

A figure emerged from the shadows — not Gideon. Older, clean-cut, suited. A glint of recognition crossed Mary's face. Her knees went weak.

"Dr. Lennox," she whispered. "From the Ethics Board?"

"Ah," the man said, smiling faintly. "So you do remember."

Mike stepped forward, instincts kicking in. "You're the one who funded the research. The behavioural studies. You sanctioned it all."

Lennox stepped fully into the light now, revealing an ID badge — not from the university. Private Sector Intelligence Liaison — Albion Group.

"We didn't sanction murder," Lennox said coolly. "But we certainly observed your choices. You were all given freedom. How you used it? That was the test."

Mary's voice cracked. "What about Debbie?"

Lennox's eyes darkened. "Debbie was an unfortunate catalyst. But her death revealed what we needed to know. Who breaks. Who leads. Who buries the truth."

Mike moved protectively in front of Mary. "So this was all some kind of simulation?"

"No," Lennox said. "This is reality. You made your choices. Now we decide how the world remembers them."

A humming noise rose — hidden cameras shifting, locking onto their faces.

"Consider this your final question," Lennox said. "Will you hide… or expose the truth and take everyone down with you?"

Mary looked at Mike.

Mike looked at the folder.

Everything they thought they understood was gone. And now, the final move would be theirs.

Chapter 30: Beneath the Surface

Sarah sat alone in her living room, blinds half-closed, laptop screen glowing dimly against the dusk outside. Her hand hovered over the mouse as her browser finished refreshing.

The decrypted server access code had worked.

She wasn't sure what she expected to find. Maybe more surveillance footage. Maybe a log of messages. What she got instead was worse.

Case File #E-2197

Title: Experimental Cohort: Voluntary Subjects — Group Seven

Keywords: Psychological Stress Index, Groupthink Analysis, Pleasure-Aggression Cycle, Subject Compliance Threshold

Her throat tightened as she scrolled through the headers. Every one of them was marked with the names of her friends. Hers. Amy's. Jane. Mike. Mary. Debbie.

They hadn't just been watched. They had been profiled. Manipulated. Studied.

Each folder contained clinical assessments — personality inventories they had taken during university orientation, archived therapy transcripts, even data from their fitness apps and campus key cards.

It wasn't paranoia anymore. It was real.

Sarah clicked open a file tagged Subject #E7–04: Sarah Ellison.

Emotional variability: High

Resistance to group pressure: Moderate

Capacity for dissociation: Significant

Liability index: 71%

She gasped and closed the window, chest heaving. Her hands shook as she grabbed her phone.

Jane hadn't responded in over 24 hours.

Mary had gone dark since the last cryptic message: "If I don't come back, trust your instincts. Find Rourke."

And Amy... Amy was likely lost or worse.

But she couldn't sit idle anymore. Not after reading what was really going on. This wasn't about guilt. Or morality. It was about control. These weren't accidents. Debbie's death had exposed a nerve in a much larger operation.

Sarah stood, grabbing her coat, stuffing a USB copy of the files into her pocket.

As she opened her front door, she stopped cold. A black sedan sat at the curb. No plates. Windows tinted dark. The engine idled, but no one got out.

Was it surveillance? Or something more direct?

She turned back, locking the door behind her, breathing harder now. The walls were closing in. Her next step had to count.

Back in the underground chamber, Mike looked at Mary, both flanked by shadows as Dr. Lennox waited, his hands calmly clasped behind his back.

The folder still sat on the table between them — the truth, laid bare in ink and blood.

Mary's voice cut the silence like a blade. "If we release this, they'll bury us."

Mike didn't hesitate. "Then we give them something they can't bury."

He reached forward, picked up the folder, and tore the camera from its bracket with his other hand.

Lennox didn't move. "You're making a mistake."

"No," Mike said. "You did."

Mary's fingers brushed the USB drive in her pocket — the backup she'd made before they came down here. Her expression hardened.

"Time to flip the experiment," she whispered. "Let's see how they like being watched."

Together, they turned toward the chamber door.

Whatever came next, they were ready.

Chapter 31: The Ripples

The world didn't erupt all at once. It cracked — in whispers, posts, and headlines that felt at first too absurd to be real.

A late-night drop on a whistleblower forum. Encrypted folders. Academic logins. University headers. Scanned memos stamped "CONFIDENTIAL – Experimental Ethics Board."

The file was titled simply: "Spur."

A journalist at The Independent picked it up first. Then a blogger in Leeds. Within six hours, it had hit Reddit and was trending on X. By the next morning, major outlets were circling like sharks.

The revelations read like a conspiracy thriller — only worse. A clandestine psychological experiment, allegedly sanctioned by a covert ethics division within several academic research institutions, targeting students in a "stress-response enhancement program."

Terms like "behavioural escalation," "group delusion," and "pleasure-aggression thresholds" were used in official reports. Dozens of names were redacted, but some leaked through: subject numbers cross-referenced with student ID numbers, vague but damning. It didn't take long for Internet sleuths to match timelines and identities.

And at the centre of it all? A girl who had vanished — Debbie Langford.

Photos of her circulated. One image — Debbie, arms around a group of students at a club, hours before her disappearance — was everywhere.

Theories spread fast.

"MK Ultra 2.0?"

"A government black-ops psy test?"

"Mass psychosis disguised as academia?"

Even those who didn't believe were glued to the story. TikTok was flooded with speculative clips. YouTubers dissected timelines. A student-led protest had already begun forming at the university gates by dusk.

The university issued a flat denial. A spokesperson called the claims "a fabricated smear campaign" based on "maliciously doctored documents."

But the more they denied it, the more people believed it.

Because the leak had included video.

Blurred. Distorted. But unmistakable: a group in masks, in a hotel bathroom. A girl lying prone. A red spatter pattern. No faces, but enough to make anyone watching feel the burn of proximity.

The public didn't need certainty — they needed a target. The university became one. The department heads another. Rumours swirled of a "Subject Zero" still alive and hiding in the city.

And in the shadows, those who had once orchestrated the game now scrambled.

Data had been scrubbed. Files deleted. But it was too late. The exposure had cracked the shell.

Somewhere in the Midlands, in a shuttered office beneath a research building long since renamed, a man stared at a monitor showing real-time sentiment analysis from across social media.

A heatmap glowed red across England.

"They triggered the failsafe," he muttered, rubbing his temples. "They're not subjects anymore."

A voice from the dark asked, "What do we do?"

The man didn't answer immediately. Then, finally:

"We adapt."

Chapter 32: Jane in the Fire

Jane stood by the window of her flat, curtains half drawn, as the city below buzzed with unease. Helicopters passed overhead more frequently now. Sirens felt less like background noise and more like a countdown. Outside, students gathered in protest — some shouting with handmade signs, others livestreaming the scene.

Inside, Jane felt like a ghost drifting through a collapsing dream.

She hadn't slept properly in days

The apartment smelled like stress — sweat, old coffee, takeout boxes that hadn't made it to the bin. Her phone buzzed relentlessly. Anonymous numbers. Journalists. Former classmates asking cryptic questions.

And beneath it all, her inbox taunted her with one unread message:

"You still think you're in control?"

No sender. No header. Just a link that, when clicked, led to a short looping video.

A figure. Masked. Standing at the edge of a dark canal.

In their hand: something small, round.

Then — the splash.

Jane had closed the browser immediately. But the image wouldn't leave her.

Was that Mike?

Was that Debbie?

Her thoughts spiralled again.

She hadn't spoken to Mike or Mary since the story broke wide. Sarah had sent one word — "run" — and nothing more.

Even the safe places didn't feel safe anymore. The pub on Derby Road, the campus café, even Mike's garage. All compromised. All surveyed, probably.

She paced.

Her laptop was open on the coffee table. Dozens of tabs filled the screen. News stories, livestreams, Reddit threads dissecting her life in terrifying detail. She didn't remember that photo being taken — the one with her laughing on someone's lap — but it was there now, shared, reposted, twisted.

"Are these the new Manson Kids?" one comment read.

"That one on the left — looks like she's loving it."

Jane flinched. She clicked away.

Her own face now felt unfamiliar. Foreign. A version of her that only existed in rumours and screenshots.

A knock at the door snapped her out of it.

She froze.

Three short raps. One long.

The signal.

She crept to the peephole. A shadow. Then a whisper through the crack:

"Jane. It's me."

Sarah.

Jane hesitated, then unbolted the door. Sarah slipped in like smoke.

She looked worse than Jane had expected — her eyes wild, hoodie soaked from the rain, a backpack slung over one shoulder like she hadn't stopped moving in days.

"You saw it?" Sarah asked immediately.

Jane nodded. "It's everywhere."

Sarah dumped her bag and pulled out a folded piece of paper.

"I followed the trace," she said. "The digital trail. Whoever leaked the files — it wasn't random. It was curated. Targeted. Someone wants us found."

Jane's mouth was dry. "Why now?"

Sarah hesitated. Then:

"Because someone broke the chain. There was a handler. And now they're gone."

Jane blinked. "Gone?"

"Murdered. Or disappeared. Either way, someone's cleaning house. And we're next."

The flat seemed to shrink around them. Rain began to fall outside, tapping against the glass.

Jane's voice was barely a whisper: "So what do we do?"

Sarah looked up, her expression hardening.

"We stop running."

Chapter 33: Blood and Echoes

The chamber walls seemed to breathe around them — damp stone pulsing with memory, the faint hum of unseen machinery vibrating beneath their feet. Mike stood at the far end of the room, staring at the ancient mural that had once seemed like myth and now felt too real. Mary was beside him, arms crossed, unreadable as ever.

He turned toward her, the air between them thick with everything they hadn't said.

"So this is it," Mike said finally. "The heart of it all."

Mary nodded. "And we're not alone in here."

The lights buzzed. Somewhere behind the steel-grated corridor, movement echoed. Not footsteps. Not mechanical. Breathing. Watching.

The platform beneath the mural had revealed more than just carvings. A panel had slid away, exposing old technology — tape reels, data drives, a console built into the stone like it had always been there. Modern wires met ancient architecture. The fusion was unsettling.

Mike gestured to the control console. "This wasn't built by hobbyists."

Mary knelt beside it, fingers gliding over buttons. "No. This predates even Morrison's network. The symbols here — they're Sumerian. But the tech? Looks like something DARPA buried in a lab back in the '80s."

"You're saying this was military?"

"I'm saying," Mary said, "we were never the first. Just the latest fools to think we were in charge."

Silence.

The weight of their decisions — the rituals, the blood, the manipulation — now looked less like deviance and more like orchestration. What they had stumbled into years ago hadn't been found. It had been left for them.

A trap.

Mike walked the room's perimeter, stopping at a wall that bore a single embedded lens — a camera. Still active. Blinking.

"We've been watched this whole time," he muttered.

Mary didn't look surprised. "And now the watchers are tightening the leash."

He exhaled, rubbing a hand down his face. "Sarah and Jane are in the wind. Mark hasn't checked in. Amy... she might already be gone."

Mary finally stood. "That's why we finish this."

Mike turned. "How? "We broadcast. Everything. What happened. Who pulled the strings. We use their equipment against them. Then we vanish before they can shut us down."

He stared at her, surprised. "You're serious?"

Mary's eyes gleamed. "We might be monsters, Mike. But I'll be damned if we're their monsters."

He smiled, faint and grim. "Alright then. Let's give the world a show."

Mary moved toward the console. Her hands moved quickly now, typing in codes pulled from memory — ones she had stolen from Morrison years ago when she still believed knowledge equalled control.

As the chamber lights dimmed, a soft chime rang out.

System Online. Broadcast in 90 seconds.

They stood in silence, the countdown ticking between them.

Finally, Mike spoke.

"When this goes out — it's war."

Mary nodded. "Then we fight."

Chapter 34: The Watchers React

The room was low-lit, bathed in a cold bluish hue cast from a bank of monitors. Seven screens played simultaneously, each looping footage from different locations — Sarah's quiet kitchen, the riverside trail Mike had walked days earlier, a grainy feed from the underground chamber. In the centre of the room stood him — the Watcher. Known only by a codename, "Rourke" was a phantom on every intelligence list and a ghost in every formal investigation. No fingerprint. No official presence. Only whispers.

Behind him, a panel of silent figures observed, faces hidden in shadow. Their silhouettes shifted only when the audio feed crackled — a whisper caught from inside the chamber where Mike and Mary stood surrounded by relics and records of events they didn't understand. Yet.

"They're close," said a woman in the panel, her voice clipped, military. "He's pushing for the truth."

Rourke didn't move his eyes from the monitors. "Let them. They'll dig where I need them to. Just like Sarah."

Another screen flickered — Sarah, her hands trembling as she held the envelope she'd just discovered in her flat. Her face was pale, sweat beading on her upper lip. The note inside had been planted days earlier — part of the push. Not to terrify her. To force her. To awaken her.

"She's beginning to see it now," said Rourke. "The whole story's never been about Debbie. That was only the start."

One of the other watchers shifted uneasily. "If they go public—"

"They won't," Rourke interrupted calmly. "They're fractured. Paranoid. And we've seeded enough doubt between them that they're just as likely to turn on each other as seek help."

He walked slowly toward a wall-mounted file cabinet and retrieved a folder. Inside: redacted reports, old Polaroids, police files with faded stamps, and a photo of a much younger Mike, not in military gear, but behind a desk labelled Psychological Operations – Deep Studies Division.

"Mike doesn't even remember this version of himself," Rourke said, laying it on the table. "But he's about to."

From one of the screens, Mary's voice crackled again — frustrated and sharp. She had found something. A ledger. A confession? Rourke's eyes narrowed.

"She's close," one of the watchers warned.

"She is," he agreed. "But it won't save them."

Silence settled over the room. The watchers knew what that meant. It was already too late for salvation. The game was simply shifting boards. Secrets were unravelling, yes — but not the ones anyone had expected. Sarah wasn't just a bystander. Jane hadn't disappeared. Mike and Mary were being guided, shaped, driven toward a confrontation with truth so twisted it might consume them.

And in the shadows, the watchers prepared for Phase Two.

Chapter 35: The Meeting Place

Sarah stood beneath the skeletal frame of the old bandstand in the Arboretum, the iron canopy rusted and flaking above her like something out of a forgotten war. Wind danced through the trees, their bare branches casting tangled shadows over the cracked concrete beneath her feet.

She checked her phone again: 10:59 p.m.

Still no sign of Jane.

The park had a strange weight tonight, as if it knew what was coming. Sarah had kept her movements discreet—switching buses, circling blocks—but she knew full well if someone wanted to track her, they already had. Still, she'd come alone, just like Jane had asked.

A footstep.

She turned sharply

Jane emerged from the trees—not from the main path, but from the shadows, her coat drawn tight around her like armour. Her face was drawn, sleepless. But her eyes, when they met Sarah's, were focused. Determined

"You came," Sarah said quietly

Jane nodded. "Because I think we're all running out of time.

They stood in silence for a moment, not quite sure how to start. Jane reached into her coat and pulled out a flash drive, holding it in her palm like it might bite

"This was in my mailbox. No return address. No note. I didn't open it at home. I didn't want to risk it.

Sarah took it gently, turned it over. Unmarked. Cold to the touch. "Do you know what's on it?

"Not yet," Jane replied. "But it's tied to Debbie. And to us.

They sat down on the edge of the platform. Sarah pulled a small tablet from her bag, powered it up, and inserted the drive

The screen flickered to life

First, a list of names. Not just theirs—but professors, admin staff, visiting scholars. Some crossed out. Others highlighted. Among them, in bold

Deborah Lowe – Status: Expunged

Sarah Blayne – Status: Pending

Jane Holloway – Status: Escalating

Sarah's throat tightened

"What the hell is this?" she whispered

Jane shook her head. "There's more.

A video file loaded next. Grainy security footage from the night Debbie died angles no one should have had access to. Camera shots from inside the corridor, the stairwell, even from what looked like a hidden lens embedded in the mirror of the hotel room

Whoever had compiled this footage… they'd been watching all of them for much longer than any of them realized

Sarah's voice was barely a whisper. "This isn't just surveillance. It's control.

Jane exhaled. "Someone's been orchestrating this. Pushing pieces. Eliminating risks. Which means… we're still on the board.

Before either could say more, Sarah's phone vibrated. One message. No number

"Your window is closing. They won't be alone next time.

No signature. Just dread

Sarah looked to Jane. "They're trying to force our hand.

"We need to warn the others," Jane said, already standing. "But not all at once. We don't know who's already compromised.

Sarah stared at the tablet screen, the cursor blinking like a metronome counting down. "Then we start with Mary."

Chapter 36: The Reckoning Plan

Inside the dim-lit living room, silence ticked like a time bomb. Sarah sat on the edge of an old armchair, Jane stood by the window peeking through the slats of the blinds, and Mary laid out three burner phones, a stack of documents, and the old leather folder.

They had everything they needed to bring down a giant—except for time.

"This," Mary said, tapping a photo of Gideon Rourke from the folder, "is the man behind it all. He orchestrated the experiments, the disappearances, the manipulation of the Blood Spurts. He seeded the myth and then weaponized it."

Sarah raised an eyebrow. "And the university covered it up?"

"Not all of them knew," Mary replied. "But enough. Rourke was one of their darlings until he went rogue. When he resurfaced last year—quietly—they brought him back under a different title. Research Consultant. Independent. Funded through private grants."

Jane shook her head. "Let me guess— those grants are just fronts."

"Exactly," Mary said. "One of them ties back to an offshore trust owned by the Everswell Foundation. And that's where we strike."

"Remind me," Sarah said slowly, "why does a philanthropic medical trust have black site servers hidden behind university firewalls?"

Mary smiled without humour. "Because it's not really medical. It's behavioural. Control. Obedience. Conditioning. Blood is just the start."

Jane turned from the window. "So what's the move?"

Mary slid a flash drive across the table. "We get this into the right hands. A journalist named Ava Linnell has been circling this story for months. She just needs proof. Real proof. Video. Documents. Audio. Everything on this drive."

"Where do we find her?" Sarah asked.

"She's staying off-grid in Newark," Mary said. "An old friend's bookstore. And if we don't get this to her by tomorrow, I guarantee someone else will silence her first."

Sarah stood. "Then we move now."

But just as they turned to leave, Jane held up a hand. "Wait."

The burner phone on the table vibrated. A single message lit the screen:

YOU HAVE ONE HOUR. STOP DIGGING. OR WE FINISH WHAT DEBBIE STARTED.

They all stared at it.

"Is this a bluff?" Sarah asked.

"No," Mary said, her face hardening. "It's a warning."

Jane picked up the drive and tucked it into her coat. "Then let's make sure it's their last."

Mary locked the door behind them as they stepped back into the night, unaware that two figures had already taken positions across the street. One on the rooftop. One in a car with tinted windows and a laptop open, watching every move.

Chapter 37: The Silent Feed

The rooftop gravel crunched faintly under the weight of the watcher's boots as he adjusted the lens on his scope. From his vantage point above the derelict pharmacy across the street, he could see the women clearly through the slit in the blinds. His breath fogged the scope for a moment—then vanished, just like everything else he touched.

"Three targets. All accounted for," he murmured, barely audible, his voice carried through the micro-comms transmitter embedded in his collar.

Down below, in the parked car with windows tinted darker than regulation, the second figure sat back in the leather seat, fingers tapping out patterns on a thin, matte-black keyboard connected to a satellite uplink. A cracked screen showed heat signatures moving in the house. No sound—just the movements.

"They've received the drive," said the voice in the car, female, sharp-edged. "They'll try to move. Should we intercept?"

"No. Let them run," replied the rooftop agent. "They're doing our work for us."

In the car, the watcher glanced sideways at a faded manila folder marked OPHELIA / ACTIVE THREADS. Inside were old photographs, snippets of surveillance transcripts, and one blood-smeared envelope sealed in plastic. She didn't need to read them again. The contents were burned into her memory.

"What about Ava Linnell?" she asked aloud, already typing in geo-coordinates. "If they're heading to Newark, she'll be next."

"She's being watched," came the answer.

A soft beep interrupted the silence. An alert lit the screen.

[ALERT: NODE BREACH ATTEMPT— SOURCE: EXTERNAL | CLASSIFIED SECTOR 7]

The woman's fingers stopped mid-keystroke.

"They're not just running," she said. "They're hacking. Mary's trying to open a backdoor."

The rooftop agent tensed. "Do we shut it down?"

"No. We trace it."

She ran a tracing algorithm, watching as the map bloomed outwards — the connection routed through six countries before looping back to a private satellite node housed in a dormant university server. Whoever Mary had recruited to help her, they were damn good. Not good enough.

"Trace complete. I've got a physical location on the uplink: northern perimeter, sector H, beneath the engineering annex. Guess where Mary used to lecture?"

The rooftop agent chuckled, dry and cold. "Poetic."

Then came silence between them. Not the quiet of failure—but the silence of anticipation. They weren't worried. They were patient. And their leash was longer than anyone suspected.

Inside the car, the woman finally tapped a single key. A command line opened:

ENGAGE SUB-PROTOCOL: INITIATE OPHELIA (PHASE II)

"Let's see how far the rabbit hole goes," she said.

And with that, the watchers didn't just observe.

They acted.

Chapter 38: Ava Linnell

Ava Linnell hadn't meant to vanish. It just became easier than explaining why she was still alive.

The laboratory lights flickered overhead as she shut down the final monitor in her private unit — buried three floors beneath the University of Nottingham's defunct biomedical wing. Above ground, the building was a carcass of shuttered halls and vandalized lecture rooms. But here, below the noise, Ava had kept working long after her name was wiped from the faculty directory.

She'd seen the signs earlier than most. The night Debbie West disappeared, Ava had been in the next building over. Her sensors — unofficial, experimental — had picked up anomalous thermal spikes, blood oxygen disruptions, and panicked vocal frequencies. She reported it once. Only once. And then, just like that, her funding vanished. So did her student researchers.

And her flat was broken into without anything being taken.

So she went dark.

Tonight, however, the silence cracked. Her laptop pinged. A code buried in a string of diagnostics blinked twice, then resolved itself into a name:

SARAH M. // OPHELIA THREAD 2

Ava stared at the line of code. Someone had activated the protocol she built to trace classified experiments — the ones buried under a program nicknamed Ophelia, a project she'd helped design before she understood what it really was.

How did Sarah get this key?

Before she could process the answer, her secondary terminal hissed to life. Grainy security footage, intercepted from a private feed — three women in a kitchen. One of them, Sarah.

She watched them argue in hushed voices. Then came the envelope. Ava's breath caught when she saw the red seal. They'd found it.

Someone was lighting fuses again. And that meant her time was up.

She swept her hand across the desk, gathering two encrypted drives, her notepad, and the small silver case she kept locked in the freezer — not blood, not tissue samples. But something worse: a cloned neural mapping drive marked "Subject X – Pre-Breach."

She slid it into her backpack and locked the room down.

As she climbed the emergency stairwell, boots echoing in the shaft, Ava's mind raced. The others — Mike, Mary, Jane, Sarah — they were all players now. But none of them knew who had been behind the original research directive. Or what Subject X really was.

It wasn't Debbie.

It was someone else.

Someone no one had noticed had gone missing.

By the time she reached the garage exit, a cold drizzle slicked the pavement. She could feel eyes on her. She knew surveillance when she sensed it. But she also knew how to vanish.

Ava slid into her rusted Saab, keyed the engine, and whispered:

"You shouldn't have sent Sarah that file. But now that you have—fine. Let's finish what we started."

The car peeled away from the curb.

Destination: the northern perimeter.

Goal: find Sarah before they did.

Chapter 39: The Watchers React

In a dimly lit boardroom nestled deep beneath a nondescript building on the edge of Nottingham, the Watchers sat in silence, eyes fixed on the wall of monitors before them.

Ava had resurfaced.

Her appearance in the Derby station's surveillance feed earlier that day had triggered every alert the system was programmed to recognize. Her face — long thought scrubbed from every traceable record — blinked back at them now with terrifying clarity.

"She's not hiding anymore," muttered Dr. Ellory, her fingertips drumming against the table.

"Or," said the man beside her, "she's making a move."

The Watchers — not a government unit, but something more covert — had spent years manipulating power behind the scenes. Universities, research labs, social behaviour studies, even surveillance networks — all seeded with their influence. Ava had been one of theirs once. A brilliant researcher, a gifted manipulator, and ultimately… a traitor.

"She's inserted herself into the mess," said another watcher, leaning forward. "The Blood Spurts group is fractured. Amy's vanished. Jane is unstable. Mike and Mary are on the verge of exposing us — and now Ava walks right into the fire?"

Dr. Ellory turned to the others. "She's not walking into the fire. She is the fire."

They all knew what that meant. Ava didn't resurface unless she had leverage — or a plan.

A different screen flickered — Sarah and Jane, walking through a shadowed corridor in the old university archives. The Watchers' access into those feeds had been spotty at best since Ava's appearance. Someone was scrubbing data in real time.

"She's already inside our systems," someone muttered.

Dr. Ellory rose from her seat and approached the wall of monitors. "This ends now. If Ava means to expose us, then we'll burn the entire project to the ground before she gets the chance. I want eyes on Mike and Mary. We need to know if they've opened the chamber."

The words were chilling — and final.

One by one, the Watchers rose. Quiet. Methodical. Ready to dismantle what they had spent years building.

Because Ava's reappearance wasn't just a signal.

It was a declaration.

Chapter 40: The Quiet Truths

The corridor smelled of forgotten paper and cold dust. Sarah's flashlight beam swept across boxes stacked high and marked only by coded symbols. The old university archives hadn't been accessed in years, maybe decades—another part of the campus swallowed by bureaucratic neglect and the passage of time.

Jane walked just behind her, one hand gripping the envelope Sarah had brought. She hadn't spoken much since they entered the building, her mind still processing Ava's reappearance, the anonymous photos, and the spiralling consequences of everything they'd done—or been caught in.

"What exactly are we looking for again?" Jane finally whispered, her voice echoing softly against the stone walls.

Sarah stopped, crouching beside a long, steel filing cabinet. "Answers. Or leverage. I think Ava knew we'd come here."

She pulled open the drawer. Inside were dusty folders—personnel files, old research proposals, and something marked Project Veil.

Jane's breath hitched as Sarah flipped it open. "Wait. That was Morrison's signature," she pointed out, jabbing a finger at the bottom of a funding proposal.

"Exactly. Morrison. Gideon Rourke. Ava. It's all tied together." Sarah laid the papers out across a nearby table. "They weren't just funding behavioural research. They were testing control. Psychological compliance. Surveillance conditioning."

Jane leaned in. "And it started with us?"

Sarah shook her head. "It started before us. But we were the latest… trial."

The sound of creaking wood echoed through the room. They both stiffened.

Footsteps. Slow. Deliberate.

They killed the flashlight. Darkness swallowed them whole.

Sarah's heartbeat thundered in her ears as the steps drew closer. Then stopped.

A single voice—deep, composed—spoke from beyond the shelves.

"Curiosity can be fatal. But perhaps it's time someone knew the truth."

The lights buzzed on. Fluorescents flickered to life.

Standing on the other side of the room was a man in a grey suit, thin-framed glasses perched on his nose. He held up his hands, palms open.

"I'm not here to hurt you. My name is Lucan. And I'm here because the Watchers have made a mistake."

Jane stepped protectively in front of Sarah.

Lucan continued, "Ava isn't your enemy. Nor am I. But what's coming—what's already in motion—needs your help to stop."

Sarah narrowed her eyes. "Why us?"

"Because you survived the experiment. And because you're the only ones left who can still think for yourselves."

He reached into his coat slowly and pulled out a sealed flash drive, setting it gently on the table.

"Everything you need to know is on this. But you only have a few days before the veil drops for good."

He turned to go, then paused. "Tell Mike and Mary to meet me. Midnight. Arboretum gate."

He vanished into the hallway, leaving behind the flickering buzz of fluorescents and a silence now thick with purpose.

Sarah reached for the flash drive.

Jane stopped her. "You sure about this?"

"No," Sarah whispered. "But it's the only real lead we've got."

Chapter 41: Between the Pines

Mike stood in the dim yellow wash of his garage light, hunched over the workbench, pretending to be busy with tools he no longer needed. His thoughts were elsewhere — circling the name Lucan like a hawk. The message from Sarah had been brief, but it was enough to stir something dormant in him.

Mary sat cross-legged on the back steps, her phone in hand, thumb idly flicking through news headlines. The world outside seemed so distant now. The scandal was spreading — whispers of disappearances, altered records, encrypted footage leaked to fringe outlets. People didn't know what they were seeing, but the fear was contagious. The Watchers had gone too far. Or they'd lost control.

"You think it's real?" she asked, not looking up.

Mike didn't answer immediately. He set down a screwdriver, then turned, wiping his hands on a rag already stained from a thousand other messes. "Real enough for Sarah and Jane to risk contact again. That says something."

Mary nodded. "Lucan. Midnight. Arboretum. Feels like a trap."

Mike gave a dry chuckle. "Everything's felt like a trap since the moment Debbie walked into that room."

That silenced them both. The weight of it hung between them like smoke.

Finally, Mary stood and walked over. "So we go in blind?"

"No," Mike said. He opened a locked drawer and pulled out a thin folder — not university files, not surveillance footage. It was his own collection, something he'd built in secret over the last few months. Scraps of data. Schedules. Intercepts. Faces and names that didn't appear in any official record.

"You've been tracking them," Mary said, surprised.

"I had to know who we were up against," Mike replied. "And now, thanks to this Lucan character, we might finally get a name behind the curtain."

Mary flipped through the pages. One name stood out: A. Kessler — a ghost in nearly every document. Approvals. Signatures. Always in the margins.

"Who is Kessler?" she asked.

"Maybe the one pulling the Watchers' strings. Or maybe just another puppet. But either way, I want to look him in the eye."

They drove through the still, cool night in Mike's car. No music. No small talk. Just the hush of the engine and the knowledge that this meeting wasn't just another step — it was a turning point.

The Arboretum loomed ahead, its skeletal trees reaching skyward under a moon-blanched sky. The iron gate was already ajar.

Mike parked and killed the headlights. They sat in the dark a moment before stepping out.

Footsteps approached.

Lucan emerged from the shadows, the same thin-framed glasses glinting in the moonlight. "You came," he said simply.

"We're not here for games," Mary said. "What do you want?"

Lucan raised his chin. "To show you where this really began. And what's coming next."

He gestured toward a hidden path between the trees.

Mike hesitated, then glanced at Mary. She gave a small nod.

They followed him into the woods.

The real story, it seemed, had only just begun.

Chapter 43: Threads of Doubt

The warehouse echoed with the sound of distant machinery—old, irregular, like the heartbeat of something asleep but dreaming. Jane stood at the edge of a metal catwalk overlooking the floor, her voice quiet.

"We're being watched again. Not just by the cameras. I can feel it."

Sarah didn't reply right away. Her gaze was locked on the wall of monitors, each screen flickering between angles of the campus, a hotel hallway, the River Trent. A looping video played silently: Debbie laughing. Debbie glancing toward the mirror. Debbie vanishing from frame.

Jane finally turned to Sarah. "That envelope you received... the note said They all lied. Who's they, Sarah? Who's lying?"

Sarah hesitated. "All of us."

She stepped forward, placing a flash drive onto the table. "I traced the metadata. Every leaked video online, every clip that showed up on Reddit or Instagram—it all passed through the same server node. Guess who's behind it?"

"Gideon?" Jane asked.

Sarah shook her head. "Ava."

Jane's heart pounded. "That's impossible. She disappeared months ago."

"She was silenced. But not dead. She's been pulling the strings from the shadows— using us as test subjects. And now she's made herself known again. That footage? That wasn't to expose us. It was bait."

Sarah turned. "To see who'd react. Who'd try to cover it up. She's watching how far we'll go."

Jane looked back at the screens, the eerie flicker casting harsh shadows across her face. "Then she already knows."

Sarah nodded. "It's a game. But it's more than that. Ava wants someone to win. She's waiting to see who cracks… and who endures."

Outside, thunder cracked, rolling over Nottingham like a warning drumbeat. And far away, a message pinged on Sarah's phone. Untraceable sender. One line:

"Next moves yours. Clock's ticking."

Chapter 42: The Clockmaker's Hand

Ava watched from the shadows of her borrowed flat, its windows blacked out, the hum of a dozen screens filling the silence. The city pulsed beyond the curtains, unaware of the storm she had released.

In front of her, five displays glowed. Each one showed a different figure: Sarah, Jane, Mike, Mary, and Mark. Their movements were logged, analysed, patterned. Every text message, every flicker of doubt—they were all part of her script now.

This wasn't revenge.

This was a reckoning.

Ava leaned forward, her fingers tapping commands into her keyboard. The timeline adjusted. New footage queued up—some real, some artfully altered. She'd learned from the best. From Morrison. From the Watchers.

But she wasn't their puppet anymore.

They thought she'd drowned in the cleanup after Debbie's disappearance. A digital ghost swept away by corrupted data and falsified police reports. But they underestimated her. She had watched from the sidelines. Listened. Waited.

Then she'd started to pull threads.

She'd seen how quickly the group fell apart under the weight of shared guilt. Not from law enforcement. From fear. From each other. No blade could carve like paranoia.

Ava clicked on Jane's feed. Paused it. Jane, pacing a warehouse office. She was close to breaking. Sarah, too—but differently. Sarah was connecting dots, sensing the larger network at play. That made her dangerous.

Mike, meanwhile, had shifted into survival mode. Still protective, still pretending to lead. But he didn't realize the camera in his garage—the old dash cam he'd forgotten to disconnect—was still transmitting.

She opened a new message.

To: The Watchers Internal Node

Phase Two complete. Activation parameters confirmed. Group under duress. External leak planted. Awaiting final response from Subject Sarah.

She hesitated. Then added a line.

Morrison compromised. Remove or observe?

A slow exhale followed as she hit "encrypt" and "send." The message dissolved into a secure packet, vanishing down the dark net's deepest corridors.

Then her burner phone buzzed.

Unknown ID. A number only three people had ever used.

She answered.

A man's voice. Measured. Cold.

"You've gone off script."

Ava smiled. "That's the point."

Static. Then:

"You realize they'll come for you now."

"They already are."

She ended the call.

Behind her, on the largest screen, the image shifted—grainy CCTV footage of Mary walking down a narrow alley, following a lead Ava had planted. The bait had been taken.

Ava leaned back, lacing her fingers behind her head.

Let them chase ghosts. Let them fight shadows.

She was the clockmaker now.

And the clock was ticking.

Chapter 45: Into the Hollow

Mary's boots echoed down the alleyway, her breath puffing white in the chill April air. The city was deceptively quiet tonight—

Nottingham's usual Friday thrum dampened by drizzle and dread. She tightened the coat around her shoulders, the envelope clutched inside its lining like a talisman.

The message had been brief:

"If you want answers, come alone. 11:13 p.m. Kingswell Alley. Bring what she gave you."

The "she" had to be Sarah. Or Ava. Or maybe Debbie, if the dead could send invitations.

Mary had told no one. Not Mike. Not Jane. Not even Sarah, who'd been growing increasingly erratic since receiving her own envelope days ago. The group was fraying fast. Everyone believed someone else was cracking.

She wasn't going to wait for another ambush.

At the mouth of the alley, her steps slowed. Her fingers hovered over her pocket—where the old USB drive Sarah had recovered now rested. A drive containing footage, names, numbers. Half decrypted. Half a curse.

The back wall of the alley was marked with a red symbol—stylized, intricate. A

Watchers' insignia, if she remembered Morrison's notes correctly. She ran a finger over it. Fresh paint.

She stepped closer.

The brick behind it shifted with the pressure of her palm, revealing a recessed handle. She pulled. A narrow steel door creaked open, revealing a descending stairwell dimly lit by a single bulb swinging from the ceiling.

She hesitated.

Then descended.

The door clanged shut behind her.

Below, the stairwell gave way to a wide chamber—half-underground, slick with condensation, the smell of rust and old electronics thick in the air. Banks of outdated surveillance equipment lined one wall. CRT monitors hummed to life as motion sensors triggered her presence.

On the largest monitor, Ava's face appeared. Static-draped. Blurred.

Mary froze. "Ava?"

The voice that responded wasn't just Ava's. It was layered, synthetic. Altered.

"Hello, Mary. I wondered if you'd come. Most people don't like seeing their file."

One of the monitors flickered. Mary's face. Then a timestamped series of images. From campus. From her flat. From that night in the hotel.

Ava continued:

"They kept tabs on you long before you met Mike. Before Jane. You were a perfect mark. Smart. Loyal. Morally flexible."

Mary's hands balled into fists. "Why are you showing me this?"

"Because you're the only one left who might still choose truth over survival."

Another screen lit up. Sarah, pacing her apartment. Mike, sharpening something in his garage. Jane, crying in her car. Mark— missing, again.

"You can burn it all down, Mary. Or help cover it up forever."

The chamber lights dimmed. A panel in the far wall slid open, revealing a pedestal. On it: a second envelope, and a keycard.

Ava's final words echoed as the feed crackled and cut.

"One door leads to the truth. The other leads home. You have five minutes to decide."

Mary stepped forward, her mind spinning. The envelope. The keycard. The offer.

Above her, somewhere in the city, her phone vibrated. A missed call from Sarah.

She didn't reach for it.

She reached for the keycard.

Chapter 46: The Quiet Pact

The rain ticked gently against the roof of Mike's station wagon as it idled on the edge of the old canal road, headlights off, hazard lights blinking like a nervous pulse. Inside, the air was heavy. Damp. Tense.

Jane sat in the passenger seat, arms folded tightly across her chest, her hair slick with rain from the sprint to the car. She hadn't said a word since Mike picked her up from the safe flat in Beeston. She hadn't needed to.

Both of them were thinking the same thing:

Who's next?

Mike adjusted the rearview mirror, catching a flash of his own eyes—red-rimmed, restless. He looked a decade older than he had three weeks ago. "We're not going to make it through this if we don't talk," he said finally.

Jane's gaze didn't shift. "Talk about what? The cameras? The envelopes? The fact that someone has footage of Amy's last breath and Debbie's last scream and is leaking it like episodes of a show they directed?"

Mike flinched, but nodded. "Yeah. All of that."

A moment passed. Then Jane pulled something from her coat pocket. A small metal USB stick. She placed it in the centre console between them. "I found it in the lining of the red envelope. Hidden."

Mike stared at it. "Have you plugged it in?"

She shook her head. "I'm not sure I want to see what's on it."

Mike reached slowly toward the dash where an old, battered laptop sat closed. He opened it. The screen flared to life, waiting.

"I think we have to."

Jane inhaled, then nodded.

He inserted the drive.

A folder appeared. Titled:

THE EYRIE.

Inside: dozens of videos. Some raw surveillance footage — of the group, of Morrison, of rooms filled with cultic imagery and ritual-like gatherings.

But one file caught Mike's eye.

"JANE_RITUAL_CAM3.mov"

His hand hovered over the mouse.

"Don't," Jane said suddenly.

He paused. Looked at her. "You don't want to know?"

"I already do." She met his gaze. "I remember more than I've let on. About that night. About the room. About Debbie."

Mike sat back, tension knotting his shoulders. "Then why hide it?"

"Because it's not just us they're after. It's not just our story. It's generations of secrets. Families. Institutions. This thing — whatever The Eyrie is — it doesn't just want to expose us. It wants to rewrite everything."

She turned to face him fully now. "And I think Mary just found the door."

Mike's eyes narrowed. "You've been talking to her?"

"No. But I got a text. One word. Kingswell."

He exhaled. "That alley?"

"She's already there. Or was. Whatever's happening next, it's already in motion."

The rain outside picked up, wind howling against the windshield.

Mike started the engine.

"Then we follow it," he said.

Jane looked back at the laptop screen. The video was still there. Unwatched. Waiting.

She closed the lid. "Let's finish this."

Chapter 47: Kingswell

The wheels of the station wagon crunched over broken glass and old gravel as Mike pulled the car into a narrow alley marked only by a rusted sign: KINGSWELL STORAGE – UNITS 1-19. Jane leaned forward in her seat, scanning the shadows cast by a flickering streetlamp. They were somewhere on the east side of the city, the kind of place long forgotten by planners and gentrifiers alike.

"Are you sure this is it?" Mike asked, cutting the engine.

Jane nodded slowly, pulling out her phone. The text from Mary was still there — one word, timestamped three hours ago. No follow-up. No location drop. But Jane had remembered the name. Kingswell had come up in one of Debbie's old notes, scrawled in the margins of her criminology textbook: "They meet beneath Kingswell. Always beneath."

Mike stepped out into the chill night air, his boots echoing on the wet concrete. Jane followed, jacket zipped, eyes scanning every shadow.

Unit 6's overhead light was out, but the padlock on the door looked recently cut. Mike bent to inspect it.

"Someone's been here tonight," he murmured.

Jane pulled the door slowly. It groaned open to reveal nothing but darkness inside. They hesitated only a second before stepping in together.

A musty, chemical scent clung to the air —
mold, old oil, dust. The unit was empty at
first glance, but in the far corner, behind an
overturned filing cabinet, Jane spotted
something half-buried in the dust: a brass
trapdoor. No handle. Just a shallow
indentation.

Mike crouched, tracing its outline. "This isn't
on any floorplan."

Jane retrieved a small metal rod from her
pocket. "Mary gave me this. Told me not to
use it unless I was ready."

Mike looked at her. "Ready for what?"

Jane stared at the trapdoor. "To find out
who started this."

The rod fit perfectly into the indentation.
With a metallic click, the panel shifted, rising
slightly with a hiss of displaced air.

They exchanged one final look before Mike
pulled it open.

Stale air poured out, cold and dry, and a
narrow iron staircase descended into
darkness. Jane went first, flashlight from her
phone illuminating the steps.

The passage spiralled for what felt like
forever. Graffiti gave way to old brickwork.
Then symbols — carved, painted, some

modern, others ancient. Each step down felt like a descent into another era.

Finally, the stairwell opened into a vaulted chamber. What light there was came from old Edison bulbs strung along the ceiling, flickering faintly. On the walls: photos, documents, red string maps — all names they recognized. The group. The faculty. Even the watchers.

And in the centre: a wooden table, and on it — a reel-to-reel tape recorder, still running.

Mike stepped forward, heart racing. He pressed stop. Then play.

A voice crackled to life. Male. Measured. British, but aged.

"If you're hearing this… the cycle has already turned again. And you've either become part of it… or you've come to stop it. Either way, you must understand: none of this began with Debbie." Jane clutched Mike's arm as the voice continued.

"This goes back to the 1974 incident. The ritual at Godshaw Quarry. We buried it. But the descendants… they kept the fires lit."

A pause.

"The Eyrie is not a cult. It is a contingency. For those who believe society must sometimes bleed to survive."

The tape clicked. Rewound automatically. Then stopped.

Jane whispered, "We weren't the first."

Mike's voice was barely audible. "And we won't be the last."

From the far end of the chamber, another light flickered on. A second reel. Another message — or another voice?

But before they could move, a sound echoed up the stairwell behind them.

Footsteps.

They weren't alone.

Chapter 48: The Man in the Dust Coat

Mike saw him first — a figure breaking through the mist, a silhouette in a dust-coloured coat moving with the unhurried precision of someone used to being watched. Jane stiffened beside him, her hand instinctively brushing the grip of the compact pistol she'd stolen weeks ago and barely remembered how to use.

The man stopped ten feet from them, the streetlamp above casting a fractured glow across his face. Mid-fifties, hollow cheeks, a scar bisecting one eyebrow. He looked like he hadn't slept in days. Or years.

"I figured I'd find you both here," he said, voice as gravelly as the cracked pavement beneath them.

Mike squared his shoulders. "You're Rourke."

The man smiled — not warm. Not even amused. Just tired. "One of them."

Jane's eyes narrowed. "Them?"

Rourke nodded toward the boarded-up church behind them, its spire a jagged tooth against the city's skyline. "You think you're running from the law, from guilt, from your own mistakes. But this goes deeper than the night Debbie died. Deeper than the videos, the bodies, the secrets you've buried."

He pulled a folded envelope from inside his coat. "This was never about any one of you. Not Sarah. Not even Amy. You were chosen because you were flawed. Willing to follow. Easy to provoke."

Mike didn't take the envelope. "What do you want?"

"To warn you," Rourke said. "Something bigger is coming. The watchers — the real ones — have activated the next phase."

Jane looked from Rourke to Mike, then back again. "What does that mean?"

"It means that after tonight, sides will no longer be a choice. They'll be survival."

Then, as suddenly as he'd appeared, Rourke tossed the envelope at Mike's feet, turned, and vanished back into the fog.

Jane stepped forward, crouching to retrieve it. The wax seal was cracked. The inside held only a list — names, dates, locations. Hers was on it. So was Mike's. So was Sarah's.

At the bottom, scrawled in red:

"Phase Two: Exposure. Let the world see what we made."

Mike clenched his jaw. "We don't run anymore."

Jane stared at the names. "Then we go to war."

Chapter 49: The List

Sarah had barely closed the curtains when the first ping came through.

One New File Received.

She stared at the screen. No sender. Just a blinking download prompt. Not a text, not an email — something deeper. Her laptop stuttered under the weight of the data.

For a moment, she hovered — then clicked.

A folder opened, revealing dozens of subfolders. All titled with familiar names.

Sarah. Mike. Jane. Mary. Amy. Debbie. Morrison. Rourke. Ava.

Her stomach twisted.

Each name opened to audio recordings, surveillance stills, redacted documents, even receipts. Not just of that night. But going back years. Conversations she'd long forgotten. Incidents she never even witnessed but had somehow been tied to.

Then she saw the last folder.

PROJECT LAMIA

Her pulse thudded in her ears as she clicked. Inside was a single video. The timestamp was the same night Debbie died, but it wasn't taken by anyone in their group. It was aerial. Infrared. High-resolution.

They were being watched.

From above.

In the corner of the screen, a watermark blinked: ARGUS SYSTEMS // ACTIVE OBSERVATION UNIT 17B.

Sarah backed away from the desk like the thing might explode. This wasn't just blackmail. This was military. Intelligence-grade. Someone had been running operations around them. She glanced out the window. Were there drones now? More watchers?

Then the message came — not on the laptop, but on her phone.

Unknown number. No text. Just an image.

It was her. Right now. Standing by the window. Taken from outside.

The caption read:

"You are the only one not compromised. Yet."

She swallowed hard. Her chest felt tight. What the hell did that mean?

Was it a warning? Or a threat?

She paced the room, breath catching. Then, against every ounce of better judgment, she opened a secure browser and started digging. "Project Lamia" wasn't something on the surface web. But in a dark database of forgotten whistleblower caches, she found one reference:

Project Lamia: Psychological contagion testing. Subject pools drawn from university populations. Controlled trauma events. Monitoring group ethics under escalating stress.

Underneath, a redacted report dated five years ago:

Primary goal: test susceptibility to ideological infection in young adult populations. Ideal environment: urban universities. Method: immersion in ritualized events, managed conflict, and manufactured moral dilemmas.

Sarah stumbled back, bile rising in her throat. They were lab rats. Debbie had been bait. The others—test subjects. The entire "Blood Spurts" chain of chaos wasn't accidental.

She thought of Jane, of Mike, even Mary. None of them had known. But someone had. Maybe Amy. Maybe Ava. Maybe whoever was still pulling the strings.

Her phone buzzed again.

MEET AT 12:00. SAME PLACE. BRING NOTHING. COME ALONE.

Beneath that, an address she hadn't seen since freshman year: the old student union basement — sealed off after a fire.

Sarah didn't wait. She grabbed her coat.

Whatever this was, it had to end.

Chapter 50: The Meeting

The room was quiet except for the low hum of the ventilation system. The industrial lights above flickered as though protesting the weight of the moment. Jane's eyes darted from the entrance to the man seated across from them — Mike, his jaw clenched tight, eyes calculating. They were waiting. For him.

A shadow moved across the glass. Then the door opened.

The figure stepped in — not masked, not armed, but calm. Dressed in a pressed charcoal coat, scarf tucked neatly, posture composed. He looked… almost unremarkable. But both Mike and Jane felt the shift in the air the second he entered.

"You're early," Mike said.

The man gave a faint smile. "Or maybe you're late."

He stepped closer, eyes resting on each of them in turn. "Jane. Mike. I expected more chaos."

"You brought it," Jane said, her voice dry.

The man — who had introduced himself as Gideon Rourke only hours before through an encrypted message — removed a folded sheet of paper from his coat. "This city is cracking open. You feel it, don't you?"

Mike didn't respond.

Jane stood. "You've been orchestrating this—watching us. The footage. The letters. The bodies."

"No," Gideon replied, "I didn't orchestrate. I accelerated what was already decaying. You're not victims. You were the match before I ever touched the fuse."

Mike's fists curled on the table. "You want to act like you're in control, but you've got your own mess coming."

Gideon paused. "Possibly. But you're still trying to outrun your own."

He dropped the paper on the table. A blurry image of Sarah and Mary — both near the edge of a river, both unaware of the lens capturing them. Scribbled beneath it: "She's not who you think she is."

Jane leaned in, heart skipping. "What are you saying?"

"I'm saying you've been focused on the wrong threats," Gideon said. "And if you want to survive what's coming next, you'll need to choose wisely."

Then he turned and left.

Silence returned.

Mike picked up the paper, staring at the image. His eyes narrowed. "Mary knew about the envelope. About Debbie. About everything."

Jane looked toward the door Gideon had exited through. "And Sarah's been hiding things, too."

Mike leaned forward, lowering his voice. "Then we stop reacting. We move first."

Outside, thunder rolled low across the sky. Rain tapped against the windows like the ticking of a clock running out.

Somewhere across the city, Sarah stood staring at another envelope. And Mary? She was no longer hiding.

Whatever came next would shatter what remained of their loyalties.

To be continued…

Final Chapter – Chapter 51: The Clearing

The fog was thick in the woods behind the abandoned observatory where the group had once gathered for their strangest rituals. Now, it had become their reckoning ground.

Mike stood at the edge of the clearing, arms crossed, watching as Mary and Sarah approached. The light from their torches carved gold out of the mist, throwing shadows that danced like spectres.

Gideon Rourke was already there — calm, hands folded, standing beside a small metal box resting atop a stone pedestal. Behind him, two masked Watchers stood guard. Silent. Unblinking.

"We're all here," Mary said, her voice hard.

"No," Gideon replied. "Amy isn't."

"Because she's dead?" Sarah asked.

"No," said Gideon, his smile almost gentle. "Because she chose her side long ago."

Mike tensed, feeling Jane shift beside him. Jane's eyes hadn't left the box. She whispered, "What is that?"

Gideon placed one hand on the lid. "The archive. Copies of everything — footage, recordings, documents. All your secrets. But more importantly… the truth about what was started, and why."

"Why are you showing us this now?" Mary asked.

"Because the game ends here," Gideon said. "You all thought this was about one girl's death. But that night… it was a door. You opened something. The consequences were never just yours."

He flipped open the box. Inside were labelled flash drives, envelopes, and a blood-red journal.

"The Watchers," he continued, "aren't monsters. They are curators. They keep records of humanity's hidden urges, failings, darkness. You all made yourselves part of the exhibit."

A beat passed. Mike stepped forward. "What happens now?"

"That depends," Gideon said. "You can expose it all. Burn it down. But understand this — the fallout will swallow everyone. Yourself included."

Mary looked to Sarah. "We could still walk away."

"No," Sarah said, stepping forward. "Not again."

She picked up the journal and thumbed through the pages. Names. Events. Dates. Not just about them — but generations. Patterns. Cycles.

"We've been part of something sick," Sarah murmured. "But maybe we can end it."

Jane touched Mike's arm. "We decide."

He looked at her. Then to Mary. And finally, Gideon.

"We bring the whole thing into the light," Mike said.

Gideon didn't flinch. "Then may you have the strength to survive the truth."

From a distance, sirens began to wail — growing louder. Police. Authorities. Or someone else entirely.

Mary closed the box. "We run out of time."

Sarah stuffed the journal into her coat. "Then let's finish what we started."

As the group turned and disappeared into the fog, the clearing emptied. Only Gideon remained. He turned to one of the masked figures.

"Activate the second archive," he whispered.

The Watcher nodded and stepped into the trees.

Because stories… never truly end.

Printed in Great Britain
by Amazon

62092463R00111